1973

THE SEVEN BOOK 3

SARAH M. CRADIT

Cover Design by Sarah M. Cradit
Editing by Lawrence Editing

First Edition
ISBN: 9781790821549

Publisher Contact:
sarah@sarahmcradit.com
www.sarahmcradit.com

PREFACE

If you're here, you've hopefully started with *1970,* followed by *1972*. And if this note looks familiar, here's where I admit I mostly plucked it "as is" from *1972*.

As with *1970* and *1972,* I feel it's important to add the disclaimer that I was not alive at any point in the '70s. I was raised on the music, values, and results of that period, coming up in the '80s with a vision of the world that matched what my parents had experienced in that pivotal decade. My musical tastes, then and now, are highly influenced by the music my parents raised me on, and even today I enjoy Pink Floyd, CSNY, Carly Simon, and other artists who shaped this decade, more than just about anything else.

Yet, as with all my stories, it's imperative to me that I get it "right." I leveraged the experiences of people who *did* live through the time, including the memories of my father, George Klepach, and my dear friend Deborah Burst, who not only grew up in the '70s, but in New Orleans, where this story takes flight.

She's been invaluable in helping me visualize those experiences unique to New Orleans in that period, such as the incredible music scene of The Warehouse (before there was a district of the same name), and the allure of the Playboy Club, for my own playboy, Charles.

Any errors, however, are entirely my own.

Beyond the setting, beyond the time, is the story, and the story is one only these characters can tell. I'm grateful they've given me the voice to find theirs.

ALSO BY SARAH M. CRADIT

THE SAGA OF CRIMSON & CLOVER

The Seven Series:

1970

1972

1973

1974

1975

1976

1980

Midnight Dynasty Series:

A Tempest of Discovery

The House of Crimson and Clover Series:

This is the recommended reading order of the series.

The Storm and the Darkness

Shattered

The Illusions of Eventide

Bound

Midnight Dynasty

Asunder

Empire of Shadows

Myths of Midwinter

The Hinterland Veil

The Secrets Amongst the Cypress

Within the Garden of Twilight

House of Dusk, House of Dawn

Vampires of the Merovingi Series

The Island

Crimson & Clover Lagniappes (Bonus Stories):

Lagniappes are standalone stories that can be read in any order.

St. Charles at Dusk: The Story of Oz and Adrienne

Flourish: The Story of Anne Fontaine

Surrender: The Story of Oz and Anasofiya

Shame: The Story of Jonathan St. Andrews

Fire & Ice: Remy & Fleur Fontenot

Dark Blessing: The Landry Triplets

Pandora's Box: Jasper and Pandora Broussard

The Menagerie: Cyler

A Band of Heather: Colleen and Noah

The Ephemeral: Autumn Sullivan

Banshee: The Story of Giselle Deschanel

For more information, and exciting bonus material, visit www.sarahmcradit.com

THE SEVEN IN 1973

Children of
August Deschanel (deceased) &
Colleen "Irish Colleen" Brady

Charles August Deschanel, Aged 23
Augustus Charles Deschanel, Aged 22
Colleen Amelia Deschanel, Aged 21
Madeline Colleen Deschanel, Deceased
Evangeline Julianne Deschanel, Aged 19
Maureen Amelia Deschanel, Aged 17
Elizabeth Jeanne Deschanel, Aged 14

For Charles

SPRING 1973

VACHERIE, LOUISIANA
NEW ORLEANS, LOUISIANA

PROLOGUE: IRISH COLLEEN AND THE SEVEN

Colleen Deschanel, known as Irish Colleen to her family and friends, peeked her head into the bedrooms of her seven children, one by one, as she did every night of her life.

Charles, her oldest, was inside sleeping for a change. She'd spent many, many nights worrying about where he was and what he was doing, but now that he was home more often, her worries hadn't subsided. A spark in her son had begun to die, and soon, he'd be married. Married to a woman Irish Colleen had no choice but to pair him with, even knowing he'd be doomed to a miserable marriage.

No one ever told her being a mother would be a constant struggle between difficult decisions and challenging consequences.

Augustus' room was still just as he'd left it. Although he'd moved into his own house, it was important to her that he always knew where home was. She'd hoped it would encourage him that he didn't always have to leave family dinners so early; he could stay the night from time to time, too. But the truth was, he'd been home for dinner twice since moving out, and she suspected he did it only to be polite.

Evangeline was gone now, too. Off to live with Augustus, for reasons that made sense at the surface, but felt more like a knife wound when Irish Colleen dug deeper. Augustus lived only a couple miles from Tulane, where Evangeline was now a student, but she would have left either way. She'd changed, and Irish Colleen had failed to see how or why, or to do anything about it. But her failure would hopefully open the door for Evangeline to explore those big things in life she was made for. She was not like the others. She was too big for their world.

Colleen's room was as neat as a showroom. Unlike the other children, who left their mark through strewn clothes or inexplicably odd posters conveying their musical tastes, Colleen's fastidious space could belong to anyone. No signs of personality to mar the neatness. Only her textbooks gave her away. The more she dedicated herself to her studies, the more sterile the rest of her life became.

She slept, though Irish Colleen had only just seen her light go off.

Irish Colleen had learned not to linger outside Madeline's door. She let Condoleezza in once a month, to dust the furniture and curtains, but the contents were exactly as Madeline had left them, when last they'd stayed over the prior summer. Irish Colleen knew this limbo was nearing an end. She would be moving herself and her youngest daughters back to New Orleans so Charles could assume command of his ancestral property, as a new husband. When she did, Madeline's belongings would find themselves in boxes, and later, in an attic.

Later. Not now. Not yet.

Maureen whispered to someone in her room. Irish Colleen often heard her daughter talking to others who weren't there, over the years, and had come to be afraid of this strangeness as

Maureen aged. She was very nearly eighteen and soon to be on her own, and this was the behavior of a child still in need of development. Yet Irish Colleen couldn't bring herself to approach this... she wasn't ready for the answers that awaited the questions.

Irish Colleen told herself to focus on the positive. God would not want her to linger on her fears. Maureen was improving in her schoolwork and was on track to graduate. Even her attitude had eased.

So she moved on.

As always, Irish Colleen stopped at Elizabeth last. Lizzy was no longer such a baby, either. She'd start ninth in the fall, and though she might never roam the halls of an actual high school, it didn't exempt her from the pains and tribulations unique to a young woman of her age. Connor, that shy but sweet boy who had been the only real friend Elizabeth had ever had, still came around, but Irish Colleen had not missed how his eyes stayed on Lizzy just a little longer now... how he watched her.

"Mama? Is that you?"

Irish Colleen broke from her reverie and stepped into the room. "Hi, darling. I hope I didn't startle you."

"No, but usually you come right in."

"Your mother is getting scatterbrained in her old age, I'm afraid."

"Mama, you're forty."

Was that all? Irish Colleen mused at this, how young forty seemed, and how old she felt. She'd lived several lifetimes, and not one had been lived for herself. "Just wait, Lizzy. Forty isn't too young for back pain and gaps in your memory!"

Elizabeth smiled. She folded the book she was reading and set it aside. "Usually it's this time of year you start to ask me about my visions."

Irish Colleen settled at the end of her youngest daughter's

bed. She hadn't consciously put a timetable on her curiosity, but she supposed Elizabeth was right. "Should I be asking you about them?"

Elizabeth shrugged. She leaned back into her bed, and as the moonlight caught her face, Irish Colleen saw the woman her daughter would one day become. Beautiful. Hardened. "I don't know if *Tante* Ophelia is right about this family being cursed, but I wouldn't have a better explanation if anyone asked me."

"You don't have to be so mysterious, Lizzy. Just say it."

"Haven't you realized, it's all so pointless?" Elizabeth rolled her head to the side. "I could tell you we were all going to die tomorrow and you'd be helpless to do anything about it."

Irish Colleen's eyes flew wide. "Are we?"

Elizabeth laughed. "No, Mama."

"Then what, Elizabeth?"

"Why do you torture yourself? What good is knowing?"

Irish Colleen's Irish temper was quick to respond, but she tempered it and gave her daughter's question serious consideration. "Helpless or not," she replied, after a thoughtful pause, "maybe I don't want you to live with this by yourself."

Elizabeth fidgeted with the hem on her nightgown. She dropped her head. "All I can tell you, Mama, is that for all the love and marriage and relationships coming our way this year, there won't be any happiness to go with it."

Irish Colleen nodded. So many times, her daughter's prophecies had driven her from the room, afraid of the very thing she'd asked for, running from the truth. But tonight she'd made a silent promise to Elizabeth: she would take whatever her daughter sent her, whether she was strong enough or not.

"Charles?" Irish Colleen asked.

"It starts with him," Elizabeth said. "But he's only the beginning."

ONE
ELIZABETH HAS AN IDEA

Elizabeth scribbled her words in a small notebook. There were few ways of sharing the burden her visions had placed upon her, and writing them down was the safest. No one else got hurt. And there was no chance of anyone ever finding the terrible pages, for she burned them once the words were out.

From there they went... well, she didn't know. Returned to the universe, she supposed, though the words never left her, not really.

Tears streaming down her cheeks, Elizabeth tore the sheets from the metal spirals and placed them in the large tin bowl. She'd stolen it from one of the kitchens at Ophélie, and now it was almost entirely blackened from her devious designs. From her drawer, she plucked the matchbook, extracted a fresh match, and prepared to strike.

Elizabeth paused in mid-action. The undisturbed sulfur burned her nose. She hated the smell, though she'd come to tolerate it.

Not this, not again.

The future can't be changed, Colleen. It just can't.

But how do you know?

I know!

Yes, but how?

"It just can't," Elizabeth whispered. She chewed her lip, tensing as she focused, willing herself to light the words on fire and release them to their new chemical form. Ashes she would toss to the wind, when the weather changed.

But she couldn't. Those words had haunted her nearly a year, hiding in her subconscious, poking at the walls to see where they were thin. Her vulnerabilities were a legion, and she feared the day they all found one another and began working in partnership to overthrow these small, but important, methods of self-care.

But how? How did she know?

And therein was the truth, formed of a glue that held her together like so many used matchsticks. *Just because. Because, because, because!* Because even if they could change the future, it would create new chaos. Her visions were the chaos she knew. She feared, more than the truth, the chaos of the unknown.

Besides, she didn't make the rules. People older and smarter than Elizabeth had tested and re-tested this theory and had deigned that the future was what it was. It was written in stone, in the stars, in whatever.

Still... she'd never talked to any of them. Not in any meaningful way. Family reunions and such, sure, but never about *this*. Her one and only conversation about this with *Tante* Ophelia had been when she was around seven and just coming into her abilities. Her mother had thrown her in the car and deposited her at The Gardens. *I'll come back when you've had some education from that woman,* she'd declared as Elizabeth stood alone upon the massive porch, wondering what the hell was expected of her.

Ophelia seemed to know the conversation was imminent, for she'd already had some refreshments waiting. Elizabeth remembered very little from that day, for most was filler and the words of an aging matriarch, but she remembered what Ophelia called *The Three Rules of a Seer.*

One, you must never seek to see what has not been given to you freely.

Two, you must never wield this power in harm to others.

Three, what has been seen cannot be changed.

These are the truths we know unequivocally, and that we live by, in order to exist freely and happily in this world, by the by. We carry a great burden, Elizabeth, but in knowing our limitations we can cease the surrender of all our joy.

If Ophelia said it was true, it must be. Elizabeth had lived hard by this belief, because her great aunt's reputation was unimpeachable. It was like questioning God, in her estimation, though she held very little belief in the idea that God was loving and benevolent. Though Elizabeth was slightly scared of her *tante,* she trusted with her whole heart that the old woman put her family before all else. Anyone who could choose not to have children because she saw her family as her charge was a special kind of human.

If only Elizabeth had been old enough and possessed enough knowledge and courage to ask questions of Ophelia back then. She'd sat, wide-eyed and awestruck as the old woman spoke, choosing each word with great care. Even if she'd had questions, she lacked the faculties to express them. But oh, did she have questions now.

And what if she showed up on the broad white porch again, this time on her own? Would Ophelia see that coming, too? Would the juice be replaced by tea or coffee? Would her words be less dressed?

Elizabeth struck the match and dropped it into the bowl. She smiled at how quickly the edges turned to black and curled inward, struggling against the intrusion and the force of change.

It felt good, sometimes, to hurt something that couldn't really feel pain.

But... what if she just *called* her aunt? There was no harm in that, right? Maybe she wouldn't even come to the phone... maybe....

All the phones at Ophélie began to ring at once.

Elizabeth tilted her water glass into the tin bowl to extinguish what was left of the smoldering flames. The paper was a mess of black sludge, though it hadn't burned long enough to turn to ash. She quickly hid it in her drawer and then waited for the inevitable visitor.

"It's for you," Maureen said, without entering. "Don't know who. Some old lady."

"That some old lady is your great-aunt."

Elizabeth could feel her sister's pause. "Ophelia? Why is she calling you?"

"How should I know?" Elizabeth lied, and was right to expect Maureen would quickly lose interest in the subject.

Elizabeth climbed to the third floor, to Charles' office. This was his place, and his alone, but he wasn't home and if she asked, he'd probably let her use it. After the door was closed tight and locked, she picked up the phone and said, "Maureen, you can hang up now."

Maureen grunted and then did as she was asked. Elizabeth waited for the click to be certain.

"Miss Elizabeth." The gravelly voice traveled like rough silk across the lines. "I've been awaiting this call."

Elizabeth pulled her knees to her chest and chewed the edge of her thumb. "You called me, *Tante*."

"Did I?" The old woman laughed. "Shall we quibble over such small technicalities, or were there other things you wished to talk about?"

"You seem to already know," Elizabeth said. "I should have guessed that."

"Your most recent visions are most troubling to you."

Elizabeth nodded as she affirmed this verbally.

"You don't have to tell me the details, child," Ophelia answered. "I've seen them myself, or enough to know why you're distressed."

"Forgive me, *Tante*, but I'm always distressed. This isn't anything new."

"Ah, yes, but it is, isn't it? What you've seen is *so* distressing that you're now questioning the beliefs you've held true all your life. And you're wondering if I wasn't blowing a little smoke your way."

"No, I would never—"

Ophelia laughed through a coughing fit. "Elizabeth, don't trouble yourself. You're right to question the things you've been raised to believe. We are all the products of what we were taught as children, and it does us no good to practice blind faith. But... I would like you to ask me. I may know what you'll say, but you will still find it beneficial to yourself to say the words aloud. Think of it as releasing them to the universe, just as you release the ashes of your visions."

Elizabeth didn't like how much of herself was laid bare to her aunt, even if she did trust her implicitly. It was like having a camera trained on her at all times, one she couldn't turn off. And how? Elizabeth's visions didn't work like a television you could switch on at will. She got what she got and never what she wanted. Never what she needed.

"Well?"

"I suppose..." Elizabeth licked at the pooling blood at the corner of her chewed thumb. "I'm hoping you can tell me why we're so certain the future can't be changed."

Ophelia made a small *humph* sound. "Every seer asks this

question, Elizabeth. Many ask it more than once, and even when they are confident in the answer, they continue to question it. I believe the future is unchangeable with all my heart, and yet I still seek ways around this truth. But that doesn't answer your question, does it?"

"No," Elizabeth said.

"No," Ophelia agreed. "Nor will words alone be enough to satisfy your curiosity."

"What do you mean?"

"Lord, do they not teach the scientific method in schools now?"

"I'm homeschooled," Elizabeth said. "But you probably know that. And yeah, I remember it from science."

"Well, then there you go. You already know the problem: you've seen a future that is great and terrible. Your hypothesis is that the future can be changed. The next step is to design an experiment that will test this theory, no?"

"I... I suppose."

"Scientists don't suppose, Elizabeth. They think, and then they act."

Elizabeth started to sweat. The air conditioning unit didn't reach into this high floor, and the conversation felt more and more like a trap she'd fallen into with her own stupidity.

"The rest isn't suitable for the telephone," Ophelia continued. "Come see me in May, when your schooling is done for the year. We will talk then and put actions to ideas. Yes?"

"Yes," Elizabeth said quickly. Her heart raced as the flush in her face deepened. "Okay, I'll come see you."

"Splendid," Ophelia replied cheerily and the line went dead in Elizabeth's hands.

TWO
A MAJOR IN DANCE

Augustus listened to the complaints of the head of his finance department with the patience of a saint.

"Stephen, you've presented your concerns to me, but I'm failing to understand how they are legitimate issues."

"She's impossible to work with! She has an idea and expects us all to listen, as if she's earned a place at the table. But if someone else has an idea? She zones out. Doesn't care a whit, unless she thought of it first."

Augustus folded his hands tighter. "Ekatherina's ideas have saved this company money."

"That's not the point," Stephen said.

"While most of yours end up costing me more."

Stephen gave a strained smile. "She needs to understand that there are ways of doing things. That there's a hierarchy—"

"If you're about to espouse chain of command nonsense, you can stop," Augustus abruptly replied. "You're good with finance, Stephen. So is she. There's room for both of you."

Evangeline, who either didn't know when her presence was inappropriate, or didn't care, sat in the corner with a smirk.

"It isn't just me who has a problem. She's pissing everyone off!"

"Her ideas are better than yours," Augustus said. He stood to signal the end of this painful conversation. "You need to find a way to work with her. That's the way it is."

Stephen ground his jaw so hard his veins at the side of his head popped. "I'll do my best."

"Yes," Augustus said.

Before he was even gone, Evangeline rolled with laughter. "Did you see his *face*?"

"I saw it," Augustus said tersely. Evangeline's weakness was subtleties, and he hadn't quite learned how to tell her she needed to leave his office, or get back to work, without offending her.

"Stephen's an ass," she said. "But he's not wrong."

"What are you talking about?"

"Your little protégé *is* pissing off the majority of the office."

"Not this again." Augustus sighed and closed his office door. "You don't have to love the people you work with. We're here to do great work. Nothing more."

"Oh, bless your heart, Aggie, I know you mean those words when you say them," Evangeline cooed. "But that's why you have me. So I can steer you back in the right direction when you miss the mark. Remember when you so generously offered to give the staff Christmas off? No? Oh yes, that was my idea!"

"Don't you have class?"

"Not on Wednesdays." Her face distorted in amusement. "If you're thinking of firing me, you can't. I'm an unpaid intern."

"I can still fire you," he grumbled. "I don't have time to deal with petty squabbling. They're adults. They need to act like them."

Evangeline rolled her eyes. "Such an idealist. If you like this girl, brother, then talk to her before she makes enough enemies that the others up and quit. Stephen's a dolt, but he's a useful dolt."

"That's foolish," Augustus said. "Anyone who would get so fussed over a young woman with new ideas is an imbecile."

"And yet you've just described the entire state of the male world, in one sentence."

"Go," he warned.

Evangeline swung on the door handle and turned her eyes on her brother once more, eyelashes fluttering. "Talk to her."

She left, and Augustus was alone to ponder the strange accusations of Stephen, and the unwelcome wisdom of Evangeline.

He wasn't running a daycare, and he refused to kowtow to the delicate emotions of the men in this office. Augustus wasn't blind to Evangeline's insight. He understood precisely why Stephen and his peers were upset, and that understanding was what made Augustus rigidly against addressing it. One of their co-workers made them look bad for their lack of innovation. If Ekatherina had shaken things up, then maybe it was needed.

So, no, he wouldn't speak to Ekatherina about her inability to minister to the hubris of the men in the finance department. Evangeline was right, Stephen was useful, but he was also replaceable.

He'd come to see Ekatherina as priceless.

CHARLES SMASHED his greasy palms into his jeans.

Cordelia Hendrickson and her father, Franz, were due at Ophélie any moment. They were actually late, a fact punctuated by Irish Colleen's nervous pacing in the parlor. He wanted to take his mother by the shoulders and bolt her to the chair. *You're making this worse!*

He didn't want to do this.

He didn't want to be here.

He didn't want to marry this woman he'd never met.

And yet, the events leading him to this unhappy event were of his own making.

Why, why, why had he, in a moment of great weakness, prostrated himself before his mother and asked what he could do to redeem himself? Why?

"Perhaps they got lost," Irish Colleen mused.

"Fucking hope so," Charles muttered and rocked forward, burying his face in his hands.

Charles had so many questions. This entire situation was bloated with mystery and truths his mother had yet failed to reveal.

For one, she'd known for years that he was going to marry Cordelia Hendrickson, when that was entirely news to him, and had failed to mention this even once. She'd even played coy initially, acting as if she'd need to "look into" marrying him off... as if she didn't already have the whole thing planned out.

And why Cordelia? Why her? There was something there, too... something fucking devious and terrible, like deals made in dark rooms. This was 1973, for the love of God! He had more money than he'd ever know what to do with, so there was no business benefit to a marriage for him. Why didn't he have a choice in the matter?

Charles imagined himself bolting from the room. He imagined letting his mother know what was what, that he was twenty-three years old and she had no right to make decisions for him. He was twenty-three and... and the heir, and a grown man, and he didn't need her constant fussing.

And yet, he didn't bolt from the room. He didn't say as much as a boo to his mother. He sat, impatiently, waiting to meet the woman who would sleep in his bed, bear his children, and either make his life interesting or terrible.

When it came right down to it, he didn't much care, either.

If he wasn't marrying Catherine Connelly, then he wasn't marrying for love.

THE WORLD WAS a blur when the guests arrived. Richard popped in to announce that the Hendricksons had arrived, and Irish Colleen turned into a whirlwind of activity, checking to make sure the tea was still hot, fluffing pillows, wiping her hands across the mahogany furniture to remove any last flecks of dust. She did this as if it was her, and not the Hendricksons, who had reason to be nervous. As if they, and not her, were from the most important family in the New Orleans area.

Charles felt ready to vomit.

New, unfamiliar voices sounded in the foyer. Irish Colleen's was almost unrecognizable as well, having climbed several octaves as she anxiously greeted Cordelia and her father, Franz.

What had Irish Colleen told Charles about this family? Next to nothing, but there were two things.

Franz Hendrickson was German-born, and Cordelia, first generation American. He was a self-made textile merchant, and the light way Irish Colleen turned up her nose at "self-made" inferred he was a bit of an upstart. Charles didn't remind her where she'd come from.

"Franz, Cordelia, please, allow me to introduce you to my most cherished son, Charles."

Charles really thought he *might* puke, if not from the growing sense of impending doom, then from the bizarre and tart-like act his mother was putting on.

"Charles," Irish Colleen warned.

He rose, for once the dutiful son, the son she wanted. The extension of his arm was robotic, and he didn't remember willing his arm to do it, but some part of him must have. He shook first the hand of Franz, and as he did, he looked up into the dour, humorless face of the man who looked at least twenty years beyond what his age should reasonably be.

"Charmed," grunted Franz.

Next was Cordelia, and Charles sucked in and held his breath until he saw her, and she came into focus.

She wasn't hideous.

That was his first thought.

His second was: there's nothing at all behind those eyes. She's dead inside.

Cordelia's handshake went no further than her fingertips. Her hands were ice-cold, and as she withdrew, she left her fingers extended, as if afraid of spreading whatever had passed from Charles to other parts of herself. She wrinkled her upper lip in what he supposed must be a smile, and the absolute pathetic failure of any personality from this woman made him want to fucking *laugh.*

Of course, the least fun and interesting woman on earth would be who his mother picked for him.

Irish Colleen directed them all to sit. Condoleezza appeared, as if on cue, and served the guests first, and then Charles and his mother. Franz sipped his tea with a polite and purposeful grace, but Cordelia made no attempt to even pretend. She curled her lip in disgust, a gesture very similar to her smile, and set it aside. A moment later, she brushed the teacup away from her, taking no chances that it might murder her.

Charles tried to imagine having sex with her, but his imagination was smaller than what the job entailed.

"Cordelia, please, tell us about yourself."

Cordelia laced her bony fingers together. Her thin lips hardly moved as she spoke, and she had a very light accent, much easier on the ears than her father's. "I went to UNO. I majored in dance."

Charles snorted tea out of his nose. "Sorry. Sorry."

Cordelia leveled a look on him so intense he forgot what had been so funny.

"I have a minor in music therapy," she continued. Then, with a hard glare at her father, she added, "I'm sure what you most want to know is how well I'll bear Charles' children. I can assure you, the women in my family are all quite fertile, and I've had my period now going on a decade."

"Glad we got that cleared up," Charles quipped, sipping his tea.

"Charles," Irish Colleen warned him again, under her breath but not quiet.

Franz laughed without humor. "What my daughter means to say, Colleen, is that when they are married they should have no complications in providing a Deschanel heir."

Charles blinked in response. *I may not be the smartest man, but I'm fairly confident sex is required to have a baby.*

"And you, Charles. Tell us about you," Franz said.

"Well," Charles said, leaning back into the chaise. "I'm not quite the overachiever Cordelia is. I'm not allowed on any college campus in the city."

Irish Colleen gasped. She reached for her neck, but had forgotten a necklace that day, Her hand dropped, helpless, into her lap.

"What a hoodlum," Cordelia remarked. "I hear some women eat that up."

"Only the women who know what they want and aren't afraid to have it," Charles volleyed back.

"So, Colleen, on the subject of appropriate dates," Franz intercepted. He cleared his throat. "We should announce in the fall. That gives us adequate time to prepare all the legal documents, contracts, and what have you. And plenty of time to plan a spring wedding."

"Summer," Charles demanded, for no other reason than his desire to maintain some modicum of power in this cattle call.

Franz lifted a brow. "Summer sounds reasonable."

"Summer is fine," Irish Colleen said quickly. "But, Charles, isn't Colin marrying in the summer? You certainly wouldn't want to steal the spotlight from one another."

"Thanks for the reminder." He settled his teacup back in the saucer. He'd never liked the shit and was tired of pretending for... for these weirdos. "They're getting married *this* summer, Mother. Not next."

"Is Colin another hoodlum?" asked Cordelia.

Franz shot to his feet. "Well, this was lovely, but Cordelia needs an afternoon nap. Colleen, shall we finish our chat while you walk me out? We can leave these two for a bit of privacy."

"Yes, of course."

They disappeared, and it was only Charles and the Wicked Witch of the East.

"So..." Charles started.

Cordelia checked her watch. "He advised to wait two minutes. Any less would be rude. Any more would be too familiar."

Charles rolled his head to the side. "Too familiar? He does know we're going to be fucking in a year, right?"

This drew the first real smile from Cordelia, but though it was genuine, it chilled him to the bone.

"Clothes on," she said. "Five-minute limits. No kissing. No talking. I'll make whatever sounds you want, but if you touch me anywhere above the neck, I reserve the right to abort with no questions asked."

"Are you joking?"

"Do I look like I'm joking?"

"Chick, you know we're stuck together, right? I didn't pick

you any more than you picked me. Wouldn't it be better if we tried to make the most of it? Have a little fun?"

Cordelia stood. She brushed a piece of lint from her wool skirt. "I'll be maintaining a property in New Orleans to retreat to as I see fit. You'll have a fair share of conjugal visits from me, at least until I'm pregnant, and then there will be no expectation of any further conjugal relations until I'm cleared to be pregnant once more."

"I guess that answers my question," Charles said.

"Good. Bye for now."

Cordelia swept from the room, rigid from head to toe, dead in every way that mattered.

He blew out a hard breath and doubled over, grabbing the arm of the couch.

"For my sins?" he wondered aloud, but no answer came, and his next thought wasn't about Cordelia at all.

It was about Cat and how much he wanted to talk to her about this bizarre exchange. How she was the only woman—only person—he wanted to share these thoughts, or any thoughts with, and wondered if she was thinking something very similar about him just then.

THE RED LIGHT ON AUGUSTUS' phone blinked for over an hour. Evangeline acted like she was his damn wife at times, checking closely the times he left the office and noting whether he'd eaten three square meals. She was exasperating. He could manage himself just fine.

The clock read past ten. As usual, he was left to close the office, with its one other nocturnal habitant. Ekatherina's soft, focused face was illuminated by her desk lamp. He could see her from his office, a direct line.

Though he had work left to do and was inclined to work all

night, he was nonetheless feeling the effects of the fatigue setting in. Ekatherina, on the other hand, showed no signs of slowing, and if he didn't kick her out each night when he went home, he suspected she would have slept there.

Augustus switched off the light in his office and closed and locked the door. Ekatherina looked up, only briefly, and then proceeded, with visible reluctance, to pack up her own things. He ended each night with the feeling he was disappointing her, when it was she who worked for him and not the other way around. Puzzling.

"Good work today," he said, though he had no knowledge of what she'd worked on that day, or most days. He couldn't have said with confidence what a day in her life at the office was like at all.

"Thank you, Mr. Deschanel." Ekatherina didn't look at him as she slid herself into her coat and made for the stairs, where they would walk down together and say their goodbyes in the cool evening air.

They stepped outside after he locked the office doors. The St. Charles streetcar rumbled by several blocks down, depositing French Quarter revelers on Canal Street.

Augustus never knew what to do with the curious intimacy in these moments, where it was only them, standing on the street, searching for the right words to part. There were many things that rolled through his mind that never made it to words. *I understand your drive. I see myself in you. I won't let them bully you from doing good work. They don't know what it must have taken for you to get here, and to prove yourself.*

"You have a nice night, Ekatherina. Drive safe," he said.

Ekatherina nodded and was already on her way as she replied, "You too, Mr. Deschanel."

THREE
WHY WAIT?

Colleen was lost to her assignment when familiar voices appeared in the otherwise soundless lecture room. Professor Green had given her a key of her own last week, when she'd mentioned offhand that she had trouble focusing at home. He'd winked as the key exchanged hands, their little secret, and she felt an indistinct little thrill pass through her. A small confirmation that she was on the right side of the table now, and that her hard work was leading her down the correct path.

"Colleen." Rory spoke first. She recognized the heavy intonation in his voice... the one that implied hands shoved deep in pockets, a sort of shame painted across his face.

"What are you guys doing here?" Colleen asked, without looking up. She sounded casual, she hoped, though her heart rate had begun an acceleration that would only rise as the conversation moved forward. The issue of focus wasn't her only reason for choosing the lecture hall to study, and to grade papers for Genetics and Molecular Biology. This was a place no one could reach her unless she wanted them to, and the question she really wanted to ask the two of them was, *how did you find me?*

"We've been calling for days," Carolina entreated. Her platform heels clicked as she stepped forward, and then stopped, further evidence of the source of her hesitation. "Irish Colleen told us when you'd be home, so we even drove out to Ophélie, twice."

"A long drive," Rory added. "Not that we mind, of course, but we really would like to talk to you about something."

"Well, you could have saved yourselves the trouble." Colleen scribbled a note in the margin of the test she was grading. *Wrong formula. Check your lecture notes.* "I've been here the whole time."

An awkward silence rippled through the chamber. "I know you're busy, but we have something we'd like to tell you," Rory said.

"Go on," Colleen replied, with a purposeful train of focus on the paper in front of her. She had re-read this student's answer four times already. She wasn't a seer, but she had an awful feeling about why her friends were here, and she'd put off this moment as long as possible.

"Can you please look at us?" Carolina pleaded. "Please, Colleen. This is hard enough."

"Hard?" Colleen played coy. She capped the red pen and placed it neatly in the groove at the head of the desk.

Carolina and Rory stepped around the desk. They stood before her, not too close, but close enough. Their body language said what their words didn't.

"Are congratulations in order? When's the date?" Colleen quipped. Immediately, she chided herself for how cutting and bitter she sounded, which was a reflection of what she felt inside, though she had no right to. No right at all. *You left him, and then you pushed him into her arms. And pushed her into his. You wanted this. You wanted this, and now you can't pine after him like an injured doe who ran in front of the car praying for impact.*

"Well..." Rory and Carolina exchanged guilty looks. "We're actually already married."

An invisible truck plowed Colleen from behind. All the blood in her face drained into her toes. She was grateful to be seated, because she had the strange and powerful sensation to sway. Married. They were married. An engagement would give her time to ease into the idea of her first love, and first best friend, united for all time. But married already... she had no time, and she was absolutely positive her first impression of the news was written clearly and in bold ink across the span of her face.

"Congratulations," she managed, mucking through the dry cotton feeling permeating her mouth.

Carolina held up her left hand to show a modest, but beautiful diamond ring. "We... uh... well, you know my family doesn't really have any money, Colleen, and uh..." She looked at Rory, but his eyes were married to his feet. "There's a lot of pressure on the bride's family to pay for a wedding. I didn't want my dad taking out a second mortgage, and though Rory's family has some money, we didn't want them paying, either."

"I see," said Colleen, grateful there was no greater response expected of her as yet.

"We didn't want to wait." Rory.

"We didn't see the point in it." Carolina.

"It's silly to go through all that planning for something you can just *do*, you know?" Rory.

Nervous laughter wove through their volleyed exchanges.

"And Rory is leaving for law school soon." Carolina.

"Soon." Rory.

"Yes, and there's still so much to do!" Carolina.

"It's easier for us to get housing if she's my wife." Rory.

"And we do want a family." Carolina.

"Not that we're in any rush." Rory.

"No, no rush." Carolina.

"Yes, why wait?" Colleen said, when they stopped their incessant rambling and turned their focus to her reaction.

"That's what we thought!" Carolina, relieved.

"Why wait for anything you want?" Colleen went on. "Why work for anything if you can just have it?"

"Colleen—" Rory, evidently without a suitable rebuttal.

"Was there anything else?"

"Colleen." Carolina this time. She leaned over the desk, and her long blond hair fell forward. Colleen tried not to picture her leaning over Rory this way in bed. She did anyway and shuddered.

"Yes, Carolina?"

"You're angry with us." Carolina's face folded into a pout. "You're angry, and I don't understand why."

"You must understand why, or you wouldn't have worked so carefully into sharing the news. You wouldn't have looked so nervous coming in here." Colleen moved her hands from the desk to her lap.

"That's not fair," Rory charged. He stepped forward and took Carolina around the waist. He looked at his wife and asked, "Can I talk to Colleen alone for a minute?"

Carolina shook her head. She wiped at her eyes. "No, anything you have to say to her now involves me, too."

"Fair enough." Rory sighed. "Colleen, you know how I felt about you. How I... loved you." He squeezed Carolina closer, a small reassurance, though everyone in the room knew who Rory's heart had beat the loudest for, even now. "I gave us more chances than you did, and your last words to me were that I should see where things go with Carolina. That we were perfect for one another."

"Evidently, I'm quite prophetic," Colleen muttered.

"You're right, we were nervous to tell you. This time last year you and I were still... well, anyway, I took your advice, and it was the best thing I ever did." He smiled at Carolina. "I love Carolina with all my heart, and I have you to thank for opening my eyes. Sometimes what's best for us was there all along."

"You're welcome," Colleen said drily.

"But you're still one of my dearest friends," Rory said. "I want you in my life. Carolina wants you in our life." He touched her belly with his palm. "We want you to be the godmother to our child."

"Jesus Christ, you're pregnant, too?" Colleen nearly leaped from her seat. But this was easier... a little. Now she understood better. A shotgun wedding. This wasn't a wedding of love, but societal necessity.

"Don't talk about it like it's a bad thing," Carolina whimpered. "We're happy. Shouldn't you be happy for us?"

"I know what this looks like, but this isn't why we got married," Rory added, insisting.

Colleen had used the past few minutes to regain control of her emotional state.

She'd found what she had most searched for, the compartment where she could store this news safely, and without easy access.

A door closed. Locked.

She stood and extended a hand to each of them. "Forgive me. I *am* so happy for you both. Truly. And of course I'll serve as godmother to your first child. What a tremendous honor."

PROFESSOR GREEN STARTLED Colleen out of her reverie. He appeared over her shoulder, though she didn't detect his presence until his hot breath tickled her neck.

"Oh, you scared me!" she cried out, clutching her chest with a light laugh.

"So focused," he replied. He perched on the edge of the desk and wagged his finger. "You're such a curious student, Colleen."

"I hope that's not a bad thing."

"Heavens, no!" He rubbed his hands over the leather elbow patches on the Houndstooth. Professor Philip Green was a man who looked plucked straight from the great Bodleian Library of Oxford. Horn-rimmed glasses framed his serious but soft-featured face. His unlined hands had never seen work outside the classroom, and his light, but commanding way of speaking made everyone around him stop and listen.

"Good." She gestured to the stack. "I'm through last week's tests, and I've just started on the tests from yesterday."

"They aren't due to be graded until next week, you know."

"I know," she said.

He leaned back on one arm and watched her. "What do you do for fun, Colleen?"

"Fun?"

"Yes, fun. Skating? Movies? Party?"

"None of those things," she said quickly, then with a smile added, "this is fun."

Professor Green's eyebrows showed his skepticism. "I am suspicious of your experience with fun if this is the pinnacle of enjoyment."

Colleen laughed. She looked down when she realized she was blushing. "I just know what I want from life. I don't let anything get in the way of my goals."

"Hmm." He nodded, still studying her. "Of the thousands of students milling about this campus, somehow I found the only one who truly deserves the honor. How fortuitous for me."

She flushed deeper. "I really don't mind at all. This helps me improve my own habits."

"You're an old soul, Colleen Deschanel. With plans bigger than the whole lot of us."

"We'll see," she replied, thinking of Scotland.

Professor Green slid off the desk. "Anyhow, I stopped in to get my briefcase, but I was thinking of grabbing a drink at the new pub on Washington before I turn in. Interested?"

Colleen's heart jumped for the second time that day, and for reasons entirely different. She shouldn't let this tenured man's flattery affect her so much; she knew that. Nor could she stop herself from comparing him to Rory, who had been her tether to her childhood world. Professor Green had seen in her the woman who sought so desperately to belong to the world she'd worked for since she was a child. Finally, after all this time, after all the ridicule from her friends, friends like Carolina, she could say, *see? This is why I lived as I did. So I could live as I do.*

Colleen cleared the thoughts away. None of this mattered. She shrugged off his polite invite, which was clearly meant to be refused.

"Thank you, but I think I'll start the drive back to Vacherie before I get too sleepy," she said.

Professor Green's smile stretched softly across his face, which had just the briefest touches of stubble. "Another time, then."

"Yes," she said, so grateful to have met him and to have him see her through the eyes she saw herself. She dreaded the term ending, and moving on. "Another time."

FOUR

#1 GUY

Balloons overwhelmed the office of Deschanel Media Group, hundreds of them. Mostly the run-of-the-mill packs of a hundred, inflated with a rented helium tank, but also some of those metallic Mylar numbers with various messages printed on their faces. *Congratulations! You Did It! #1 Guy! You're a Winner!*

Evangeline had been rolling her eyes so hard all morning that she had a headache. The busybody secretaries were responsible, of course. They'd called no less than four meetings in the boardroom about the party, squirreling themselves away with giggles and whispers and signs reading DO NOT ENTER when they were inside.

"Fuck off," Evangeline whispered whenever she passed by their trite acts of subterfuge planning. The middle-aged women—the DMG Sewing Circle, as Evangeline thought of them—either didn't understand the head of the company employing them *at all* or they understood all too well and thought they were being cute.

Some jackass nearly scared her off her feet by blowing a kazoo in her ear as she passed. "Ah, fuck off, John," she hissed, her new mantra. She'd co-opted the word fuck into her life the way someone with more warmth might embrace a foster child.

Her own desk was covered with confetti, and Evangeline thought to herself that she would commit murder for less.

But, for all of her annoyance... for all of Augustus' annoyance... it hadn't been lost to Evangeline that everyone else *was* having fun. They'd earned this celebration, which wasn't just for the CEO, but for all of them, because they'd all been part of this journey.

Volume Six of Deschanel Magazine was printing in two weeks, and this time, in forty cities and towns across the state of Louisiana. On top of that, Augustus was gearing up to sign a deal to bring the magazine to three more states by winter: Mississippi, Texas, and Georgia. The office had every reason to celebrate, and celebrating they were.

The only one missing was the guest of honor.

Evangeline meandered through the finance area on her way to check on her brother. She didn't need a crystal ball to know exactly how she'd find him: shades drawn, head down, working on the next moment instead of experiencing the one he was in.

She grunted as she tripped and took four steps to right herself, catching her hand on the edge of a file cabinet. Looking back, she saw the culprit... a handbag, sitting too close to the aisle, instead of in a drawer, where it belonged. Then came the soft apology.

"I rearrange my desk. I didn't mean to cause trouble." Ekatherina enunciated each word slowly and clearly, working to reduce any sign of her strong Russian accent.

"Yeah, okay. It's fine," Evangeline said. She rubbed her knee, which had hit the metal cabinet on her way to saving herself. "Everything going okay with all you math geeks?"

Ekatherina's mouth twitched. Her spine stiffened. "Your brother's business performs very well. He asks me for advice.

Investments. I give him advice, good advice. He appreciates my advice."

"You're giving my brother direction on where and how to spend his money?"

"Yes, I know much about this, too. Your brother's margins earned him back his investment and then some. He will be a very rich man. He needs someone like me so he doesn't lose it all."

Even taking into account Ekatherina's clipped English, Evangeline suspected there was far more at hand than what was being said. She hadn't really considered that, to do her job, Ekatherina would need access to confidential and provocative information, like her brother's income. Her interest in it was clear... it was the first thing she said when asked about her job, and Evangeline knew your first answer to a question hit closest to the truth.

Augustus had worked too damn hard for some gold-digging opportunist to slide in and swindle him out of everything. He'd also lost too much to survive another significant disappointment.

She ground her teeth. Telling Augustus her concerns had created a bit of a rift between them, one she didn't like at all. She could live with it, if he listened and exercised more caution, but he rarely did. He was a man with few blind spots, but Ekatherina Vasilyeva was a big one.

Evangeline would need to find a way to handle this problem on her own.

"Hey, you've been here six months now, right?"

Ekatherina nodded. Her cheeks were still aflame from the horror of tripping her boss' sister, though any other woman in the office would have blown it off already. Evangeline wondered if purse-tripping was a capital crime with a trip to the gulag back home.

A flicker of an idea passed through her mind.

She stole a half-drunk flute of champagne from a nearby table and toasted her. "I guess we're not done celebrating then."

"Thank you." Ekatherina hung her head meekly, but as she did, Evangeline caught the fire in her eyes, and the grin she struggled to hide.

Her disdain for Augustus' pet burned hotter than ever. This "contrition" was no more than an act, meant to disarm. It had almost worked on Evangeline, until she pressed just a bit at the surface, to find what she'd been looking for.

Augustus believed Evangeline was going to MIT in the fall. Hell, Evangeline believed Evangeline was going to MIT in the fall.

But her work here wasn't quite done, and days like this put this into finer emphasis.

"Hey, Ekatherina, question."

The young woman looked up. She regarded Evangeline with her wide doe eyes.

"Your work VISA that we're sponsoring. When's it up?"

"December."

Evangeline nodded. Smiled. "Right. So you only have six more months."

She pivoted and left the little tart's reaction to her imagination.

AUGUSTUS SHOULD HAVE JOINED them for the celebration. They were all here because of him and his vision, and their hard work and belief in that vision had put his magazine on the map. A good leader would be clinking glasses and shaking hands. Delivering individual anecdotes to each of them, to show he'd paid attention and what they'd done mattered to him.

He was ashamed to admit himself incapable of these social graces. He'd hoped that would change with age, as he grew into the businessman he'd worked to be, but the opposite had happened and he feared he was heading down the path of a recluse. He couldn't remember the last time he'd even been home to see his mother. Worse, he'd blown her off this week when she was in town looking for homes. He was supposed to help. He told her he had to work.

It wasn't a lie. Nor was it the truth simply because of all the work to do. The best thing Augustus had done for his business was hire the right people, and because of them, he *could* have gone home every night on time, had he wanted. But he needed to work, because it was the only way he knew how to feel alive.

Augustus didn't know what was wrong with himself. He didn't have the energy to dig deep enough to find out.

The party had died hours ago, and then the revelers had all retreated to their homes, their families. There was a world beyond these doors, but Augustus preferred the comfort of night, both stepping in and out of the office when darkness was still king.

He packed up his briefcase and turned to leave when a figure in the door startled him.

Augustus stared at her. He presumed she was like him, always preferring things just so, and he couldn't think of a single night when she'd come to see him first. This wasn't how things were supposed to go. He would grab his things, lock his door, then pass by her desk to escort her out.

"Sorry if I scared you, Mr. Deschanel," she said. She held her bag in both hands, and it was half as big as she was. She practically drowned in her too-big blazer with the shoulder pads that made her resemble a linebacker.

"No, you're fine, Ekatherina," he said quickly. "Do you need anything?"

"Usually we leave at eleven and it is almost eleven thirty. Is everything okay?"

"Of course it is." Yet she was right. He was thirty minutes

behind his usual schedule, and that was unlike him. He chalked it up to the chaos of the day. Tomorrow would be back to normal.

Augustus approached the door and she didn't move. He didn't want to be rude, but she blocked his exit. When she realized, she stepped back several steps with a guilty look.

He locked the office and they moved through the office, toward the stairs, as they did every night, except this night was different. She'd come to him. He was late.

His heart raced. He felt sick at how such a small wrinkle in his routine had set his anxiety on fire.

Once outside, Ekatherina did one more thing that was atypical. Instead of her perfunctory good night, she attempted conversation.

"I do not think your sister likes me."

"Evangeline?" Of course it was Evangeline, but how else could he wrap his mind around how unusual her words were? She never asked him anything and never offered what wasn't asked. Everything between them was scripted, like all things in his life.

"Da," she said, then shook her head. "I mean yes. She thinks I cheat you of money."

"She said that?"

"I try to explain I only want to help you, but I do not think I say it right."

Augustus sighed into the cool spring night. "Don't worry about Evangeline. She's protective and lacks delicacy. I wouldn't ask for your help if I didn't value your experience."

"Really?"

The innocence in her eyes as the question hit her lips brought a smile to his face. "Yes, really."

"That is a relief." She breathed out a furl of white air.

He touched her arm. "If there is a concern with your ethics, or performance, I won't send my sister to tell you. I'll tell you myself."

"I know I am silly sometimes," Ekatherina said. "But I do not want to be. I take pride in my work. I take it very seriously. I only want to make you happy."

"You do," Augustus said. Then and only then did he realize the tone of the conversation had shifted. "Well, I best be off."

"Da. Yes, me as well."

He started to wish her a good night and then decided to ask the question brewing in his mind for months. "Ekatherina... your family. Have you seen them since you came to the United States?"

Her eyes shifted away. She wasn't prepared for the question. "No, Mr. Deschanel. I cannot afford to bring them here. But I save money and I will do as I promised and bring them all here."

Augustus wanted to ask her more, but he'd seen how painful even the cursory question of her family had been.

Whatever he wanted to know, he'd need to discover on his own.

"Good night, Ekatherina."

"And you, Mr. Deschanel."

FIVE
TO CHANGE THE FUTURE

Ophelia watched Elizabeth drink her sweet tea with a hawkish grin.

"Weather is warming fast," she said. "Drink up."

Elizabeth, whose imagination was ordinarily on par with that of her uninspired mother, ran through a series of sequences on how this meeting would go, many of which ended up with the tea containing a rare and untraceable poison. In at least one version, Colleen saved the day by running her baby sister's blood through a lab and producing the damning evidence at the funeral with all the dramatic flair of a Matlock courtroom.

Ophelia laughed. "You are your father's daughter. Always worrying about the wrong things."

"How do you do that? See things so quickly?"

"That wasn't my third eye, child. I read your mind. Hasn't anyone taught you to block?"

"I know how to block," Elizabeth defended. The problem was, she'd grown lazy about it over the years. Most of her family left her alone, and blocking was too exhausting to maintain if it wasn't needed.

"Don't trouble yourself assembling one for my sake. I'll agree to stay out of your head for now." Ophelia chuckled again. Her long white hair was pinned in a soft chignon at her neck, and it was still as thick as ever. Elizabeth marveled at her nonagenarian aunt, who was somehow both ancient and ageless at the same time.

"But you do see things like that... mundane things. You saw I'd call you."

"I did."

"How?" Elizabeth shook her head. "I only see big things. The awful things usually, that I wish to God I hadn't. But I don't see Mama going to the store, or the score of the baseball game. I can't complete anyone's sentences."

"Nor could I at your age," Ophelia answered. "And you might never. Time will tell. Everyone's gifts unfold at different rates, and in different ways. Yours might go away entirely. No way to know."

Elizabeth smirked. "I'll bet you do know."

Ophelia returned the look. "I just might. But I won't divine your future, Elizabeth. I've done it for others, but never for seers. The singular reprieve a seer has is that the one and only future they can't see is their own. It's what keeps us from going entirely mad."

"I feel like I've gone mad."

"Only some," Ophelia said. "See your own future and you'll be lost to it."

"So you don't know your own future?"

"You're asking if I've seen my death, I suppose, since there's not much more to look forward to." Ophelia coughed into a silk handkerchief, then tucked it into her blouse. "I have not. I would've never fathomed I would live as long as I have, that I'd outlive all the others, and I've no inkling of what I have left. I'm happy to keep it that way."

Elizabeth set her sweet tea on the white lattice table. Her finger wiped at the condensation, tracing lines around the edges of the glass. "You said you could help me."

"I don't believe I used those words. I wouldn't promise such a thing. But I do have a way that will help you move forward, one way or another."

"Tell me, please, *Tante*." If there was a chance, however remote, she could help her family with what lay ahead, she would do anything at all.

"As I said on the phone, you have an experiment ahead of you. Your hypothesis is that the future can be changed."

"I don't *know* if it can be changed," Elizabeth argued. "I just want to try. I have to try."

"Of course. As we all did once." Though the temperature was in the eighties, even sitting amongst the flora of the screened-in porch, Ophelia settled her shawl tighter around her neck. "Does your mother know why you've come to visit me?"

Elizabeth shook her head. "I said I was worried about you after you were so sick. She said I could stay for a couple hours while she does her errands here in town."

"Colleen has never liked me," Ophelia said. "I suspect she regrets marrying into this family. But she does not regret you children, and for that, I can stomach her bullishness. It goes without saying that she will not support you in performing this experiment, then."

"No," Elizabeth agreed. She almost laughed at the idea of her mother helping her with anything of the sort.

"You're not yet old enough to drive yourself," Ophelia noted, thinking to herself. "You'll need an accomplice, though not a very well informed one, I should think."

"An accomplice?"

"Your experiment will be here, in town. In New Orleans.

Two days from now, in fact. You'll require a ride into town, one that will not be so discerning on your whereabouts."

"I'll figure that out," Elizabeth said. "What's the experiment?"

"Two days from now, a paddlewheel boat will collide with a tanker on the Mississippi, as they pass the crescent in the river. The tanker will fare well in the crash, but over a hundred of the twelve hundred passengers aboard the Cajun Queen will perish."

"Jesus."

"Not on the manifest."

Elizabeth's mouth twitched at the odd joke. "Okay. And what do I do?"

Ophelia held out her bony hands. "Whatever you think you can do to stop the Cajun Queen from launching on time. Her departure time is set for 12:15, and the tanker will collide at 12:37. You don't need to stop the ship altogether, just delay it long enough for the tanker to pass without incident. A single minute should be enough."

Elizabeth pressed her sweaty palms down the length of her corduroys. This was it... the idea was brilliant. She didn't need to do much at all, just give the captain or the passengers enough of a distraction to delay their terrible fate. A minute or two. Five to be safe. Maybe she'd feign an illness. Hell, she could sing and dance for five minutes if she had to.

"I can do this," Elizabeth said. "It doesn't sound so hard."

Ophelia's thin lips stretched into a knowing grin. "I suppose we'll see, won't we?"

"ELIZABETH." Connor stood in the door to her room, wearing a look meant to be serious. "Maybe there's another way."

"You don't have to come."

"Don't be like that."

"Like you're being? You know why this is important. *You,* more than anyone."

"I'm just thinking of all the ways this could go wrong."

"Like me saving the lives of a hundred people? How horrible!"

He groaned. "No, like it *not* working, and the police getting called on the teenage meddler trying to stop a ship from leaving port. How will you explain that to Irish Colleen?"

"I'll say I was drunk."

Connor laughed. "You need a better imagination."

Elizabeth glared. "You coming or not?"

He stepped out of the way. "After you, I guess."

MAUREEN CHECKED on the kids through the rearview mirror. Elizabeth and her little friend weren't really kids anymore, but she fancied herself the older, more mature sister, swooping in to save the day.

Though she'd had her driver's license now a few months, Irish Colleen never let her go anywhere, except into Vacherie for groceries. But Irish Colleen was in New Orleans for the day visiting her family, a twice annual tradition that never involved her children, and wouldn't be back until late into the evening. Maureen would be back at Ophélie long before the woman ever realized one of the cars was missing.

Maureen didn't *really* believe Elizabeth and Connor were attending a birthday party in Mid-City. Connor, maybe, but Elizabeth had no friends except the shy boy fidgeting nervously beside her in the backseat. And besides, Maureen knew her sister. The city was the last place she wanted to be. She clammed up and looked green in the face anytime they went into town for anything.

But Elizabeth had been plucked from the school system at a

delicate point in her young life. She'd never had the chance to *live* the way Maureen did, and that was very unfair, as she saw it. So if Elizabeth wanted to get into a bit of mayhem, Maureen was happy to help facilitate.

Elizabeth promised Connor's mother would have them back to Vacherie by eight. Maureen didn't doubt this; the only thing Elizabeth feared more than her crazy visions was Irish Colleen's wrath.

Maureen dropped them off in front of a house on Bienville. The backseat arguing over which house it was didn't increase her confidence that they were up to any good, but she enjoyed the idea of Elizabeth misbehaving. And there was no harm in it... Elizabeth, of all of them, was the most cautious, because she saw clearest what the horrible outcomes could be for those who didn't tread through the world carefully.

"All right. Don't have *too* much fun," Maureen said as they stepped onto the sidewalk and looked confused and surprised at the neighborhood they'd landed in, which was unlikely to house any friends of theirs. *Next time, research better, kiddos.*

She sped off, satisfied that she'd both checked off the box marked *Good Sister* and had a little rebellious car-stealing adventure of her own.

ELIZABETH MOPPED at her brow with the back of her arm. The day was a scorcher, just one of many details she hadn't thought of when she tried to misdirect Maureen with a fake address on Bienville.

She should have known: Maureen didn't care. Maureen would have taken her right down to the pier and still not asked any questions.

The three mile walk to the French Market was grueling. Connor whined about all the great injustices of the act for the first mile and then stopped, seeming to appreciate the merits of conserving energy. By the time they climbed the levee behind Jackson Square and ascended the riverfront, she'd lost almost all desire to do what she'd worked so hard to do.

"Where is it?" Connor asked.

"There's a map over here," she said. She ran her finger down the glass. "Cajun Queen should be just down there."

Elizabeth glanced at the Timex she'd gotten for Christmas. It read 12:10. Guests would be finishing boarding, and they'd be pulling away in only a few minutes.

She broke into a jog, and Connor, after a hesitated grunt, followed. She wove through the crowds gathered along the riverfront as they drew closer to where the old paddlewheel held court.

They came to a stop right outside the ticket booth. "We only have to delay them. That's it. Remember Plan A and Plan B, or do we need to go over them again?"

"I remember." Connor looked like he might lose what was left of his lunch.

"I don't think we'll have a lot of time to make this work, so I'm going to start as soon as I see the captain head back up the boat ramp." She pointed at the old man whose uniform made him clearly identifiable. He spoke with someone from the port authority, sharing a glance at paperwork. "It's *him* we need to distract. If we end up getting someone else's attention, he'll just go about his business, and then all those people die. Got it?"

"I don't feel good about this."

"I can tell."

"Plan C is me running to call for help if something goes wrong."

"No," Elizabeth said firmly. "There is no Plan C, Connor. Plan C is we *fail*, and I can't fail at this! Do you understand?"

His throat bobbed as he swallowed. "I understand."

Before he could express any further hesitation, Elizabeth announced she was going, and she ran toward the captain, arms flailing.

"Help! Help me! This man is trying to kidnap me!" She gesticulated wildly toward the crowd gathered by the nearby brewery, careful not to point at any one person. She tugged at the captain's arm. "Please, you have to help me!"

The captain's eyes traveled between his ship and the desperate girl hanging off him. "Well, now, it's okay, miss. That's not going to happen." He patted her head and looked past her. "George! Can you take care of this? Don't let her out of your sight."

The man in the ticket booth rushed from his post and over to them. "What's happening? Did she say someone tried to kidnap her?"

The clock read 12:13.

Shit. "Please," she pleaded with the captain. He patted her on the head once more and then gently peeled her away.

"George, call her parents and get the police involved if need be. We're fixing to be late here." He made his way up the ramp.

Elizabeth didn't look at Connor. He didn't like this next part, Plan B, and if she caught his eye she might lose her courage.

As a young girl, she had a transient heart problem that caused her to frequently faint. Once they identified the issue, Colleen and Evangeline healed her, and the fainting spells stopped. But Elizabeth never forgot the physical circumstances leading to the spells, and long after her body no longer needed to, she continued to employ this now-learned skill to extricate herself from stressful situations. Problems in school, namely.

When her sisters found out, they made her promise never to do it again. Colleen, especially, who told her any loss of oxygen to the brain could cause irreversible damage. *You're playing with fire, Lizzy. Some things can't be healed.*

Elizabeth closed her eyes and built up the panic within her. Familiar spots appeared before her eyes. That terrible lump in her chest. She managed to grab the captain's sleeve on her way to the ground, but the fabric slipped through her fingers, and she remembered nothing after that.

The next thing she saw were Connor's teary eyes hovering over her.

"You were out for two minutes," he moaned. "Two! I didn't know what to do... I was so scared."

She rolled her head to the side. George was back in his booth, with a phone to his ear, eyes trained on her. Some tourists had flocked to their side as well and formed a protective circle around her and Connor.

But nowhere did she see the captain.

She tried to turn toward the river and the ship, but the crowd blocked her view. She groaned and tried to roll herself forward, but there were hands all over her, trying to keep her still.

"Connor... where is he? Where's the captain?"

"Lizzy, you were out two minutes!"

"Connor!"

Connor bowed his head. "He went with the ship. It just left port."

"Late?"

"No. My watch read 12:15:02. Not late."

Elizabeth opened her mouth as wide as she could and screamed into the humid air.

SHE DIDN'T KNOW what Connor had said to get the gathered Samaritans to let them walk away. She didn't care.

Mercifully, they were long gone before the fateful 12:37 collision.

Elizabeth walked several paces ahead of her best friend. He

didn't ask her where they were going. He seemed to understand she had nothing to say, about that, about anything. Her heart was a mess.

She didn't think of Ophelia, and having to face her with her disappointment. It was worse, knowing her great aunt already knew she'd failed; had known she would fail before she even tried. Ophelia had surely seen that the captain intent on sailing on time could not be swayed. His ship was always destined to be on time, and that punctuality, on this day, was always meant to be the end of a hundred lives.

But she had to try. She had no choice. To not try would be to surrender the piece of her humanity that no normal person possessed; the one unique to seers that allowed them to survive the things they were forced to witness.

Elizabeth hadn't known where she was going until she got there.

She stepped through the back gate of Oak Haven and went around to the porch, which was empty now, but still home until the Deschanel trust granted it out to some other family member. She still felt a pull to the old gray paint and the plaster columns. Here, she'd invented the games that kept toddler Elizabeth from losing her mind. The games that blurred fantasy, reality, and an unchangeable future.

Elizabeth curled into a ball and closed her eyes.

Moments later, she felt Connor settle in beside her. He placed one hand on her back, leaned his head against the side of the house, and they stayed like this, in silence.

MAUREEN THOUGHT she'd seen Irish Colleen mad, but her mother was bringing furious to new heights.

"She said she had a ride home," Maureen whined and wished

she'd just said nothing at all, because this was so much worse. She'd severely miscalculated Elizabeth's intentions, whatever they might be. No one knew, because no one could find her, and now she was missing.

This was what Maureen got for trying to be a helpful big sister.

What she got for letting her guard down at the first sign of her own happiness.

"Get in the car. Now."

"But Charles and Augustus are already out looking for her." It wasn't that Maureen didn't want to help; it was that she was afraid. She'd begun to wonder if Elizabeth had fallen victim to something horrible. There had been news of a serial killer in Baton Rouge, and now they were saying he'd struck in New Orleans, too. The victims were all young girls, between the ages of ten and twenty. It was too terrible a thought, but if she buried her head in the sand, it couldn't be true.

Then again, if something *had* happened to Elizabeth, Maureen would probably be the last to know.

Connor's parents, Savannah and Jamie, had been calling nonstop for hours. That's when Maureen knew for sure things were not all right. Savannah was supposed to be their ride home, but knew absolutely nothing about it. She thought Connor was with Elizabeth, safe in Vacherie.

"And Colleen, and Evangeline," Irish Colleen answered. Her face was a mosaic of rage and disappointment. "What the *devil* were you thinking, Maureen?" She whipped her head. "Don't answer that. We both know you weren't thinking a damn lick."

"Mama, I'm *sorry*. I was only trying to help."

"We need to have a firm lesson when Elizabeth is home and safe about the difference between helpful and foolish. Now, *come on*."

ELIZABETH AWOKE to the sound of footsteps in the grass. She shook Connor as a shadow fell over them.

Augustus sighed in heavy relief. "Lizzy. Thank God."

He ascended the stairs and knelt down before the two of them. "And you, Connor. Your mother is a mess."

"My mother couldn't care less."

"That's not true," Augustus said. He reached his arms forward and slid them under Elizabeth, lifting her like a rag doll. She didn't resist; her face instinctively curled into his chest like an infant seeking succor. Her body rolled inward as he held her.

"Where are we going?" Connor asked. He followed behind them, back to the street, where Augustus' car sat idling.

"I'll drop you by your house before your mother has a heart attack."

"And me?" Elizabeth asked.

"We'll go to Magnolia Grace and wait for Mama and the others to come by. They've been out searching for hours, Lizzy. Where *were* you?"

"You wouldn't believe me if I told you."

"I might," he said, settling her into the back seat. The dome light illuminated his worried face and she saw just how scared he was; how scared they all must have been. In trying to help, she'd made things even worse.

"You don't have to tell me." He pulled back. "But you do need to think of a story that Mama will believe. I'm guessing the truth is out of the question here."

"It is."

He checked his watch. "We all agreed to meet at my house at midnight to check in on how the search was going. That gives you thirty minutes to think of something compelling."

"Thanks, Aggie." Of all her siblings, she expected his silent collaboration the least.

"We do what we have to do in this family, Elizabeth," he said and slid into the driver's seat.

He said nothing else as they drove quietly through the sleeping Garden District.

SUMMER 1973

VACHERIE, LOUISIANA
NEW ORLEANS, LOUISIANA

SIX
MADE IN THE USSR

Augustus locked his office door. He never did this, not during business hours, but the staff had become familiar over the past months and had forgotten the need for knocking. Right now, he needed guaranteed solitude.

He wasn't technically doing anything wrong, and he'd told himself this very thing, first as he hired Jamie Sullivan to help with the background check, and later, as he tried to come about the information more directly, through Ekatherina herself, with no success.

There wasn't as much information in the manila envelope as he'd hoped for. It wasn't much of a packet at all, just a few pages collated with a small-sized paperclip.

She was born Ekatherina Aleksandrovna Vasilyeva, in 1950, in an unnamed village outside Leningrad. Ekatherina's father, Aleksandr Vasilyev, born 1930, was a ranking member of the Communist Party and a loud voice for Marxism, until 1970, when he spent a year in the gulag and then, miraculously, released but out of favor. Augustus flipped through the handful of sheets, looking for more information on Vasilyev's fall from grace, but there was nothing more written about it.

Ekatherina's mother, Elena, maiden name Kozlova, born 1932, labored in a factory for years before landing a job as an interpreter for the Kremlin in 1965, but lost that coveted job when her husband was arrested in 1970. She returned to the factory for a short time until her husband was released in 1971. There was no record of her employment beyond that point, and the investigator presumed she continued from that point as a housewife.

Ekatherina was the oldest of three siblings. Her brother, Aleksandr, was born in 1955, and a younger sister, Anasofiya, in 1960.

There was not much more about Ekatherina's family. Only that the young sister, Anasofiya, had been battling a long-term illness.

Ekatherina applied for her au pair VISA two months after her father's imprisonment. She flew to New York in January of 1971, where she stayed for a few days, and then to New Orleans, where the Connelly family took her in, and she worked for them up until she came to work for Augustus in the winter of 1972. There was also mention of the business school Connelly had paid for her to attend. She'd quit upon accepting employment at DMG, but now Augustus wondered why she hadn't continued. Perhaps she didn't think he'd allow for such flexibility in her schedule.

Augustus slipped the papers back in the envelope. He pressed the brad flat and laid the file upon the desk, spreading his palms across it.

Russia. The communists could call this ancient country whatever they wanted, it didn't change what a place really was. New Orleans had changed hands more times than he remembered from history, from French, to Spanish, to French, but this city's identity hadn't wavered. Leningrad, which had not even fifty years ago been Petrograd, had for most of its history been St. Petersburg. One of the few classics Augustus had ever enjoyed, *War and Peace,* had captured his vision of the city forever, of sparkling lights and masquerade balls at the Winter Palace; the bravery of Tsar Alexander I as he faced off against Napoleon.

Much had changed there since then. Lenin, Marx, Stalin, the Bolsheviks. Brezhnev was only the latest in a long line of Chairmen who had upheld the colorless and dispiriting legacies of stripping the life and history from the Russian people. Augustus knew enough about communism to understand it was the perfect embodiment of a good idea that never had a chance of being successful as long as men were prone to corruption.

Why had Ekatherina's father aligned with the Communist Party? Out of fear? To protect his family? Perhaps, he, too, had read Marx and Engel's *Communist Manifesto* and seen a better world. But then why had he fallen out with them?

Of one thing, Augustus was convinced. Ekatherina's timing of leaving her mother country was not coincidence. Nor was the way she kept to herself, politely but always refusing invitations from her co-workers for anything social... kind, but never friendly. It wasn't his business what she did with her money, but she wore the same five outfits each week, and he could see where they'd begun to wear.

Somewhere, someone had told him it was illegal for the Soviet immigrants to send money back to their families in the USSR. It upset the careful balance the Communist Party sought to maintain with their policies and led to unplanned inequities.

And what had she said, the one time he'd worked up the courage to ask her about her family?

No, Mr. Deschanel. I cannot afford to bring them here. But I save money and I will do as I promised and bring them all here.

Augustus wondered how many opportunities existed

between the nations, that would have allowed her family to come with her. Was au pair the only option? Anasofiya, the young sister, was *too* young, but perhaps that would become an option for her as well. But the parents? The son?

If money was all that was needed, there would be many more immigrants from the Soviet Union living and working here. Of that Augustus was almost certain.

Augustus had something Ekatherina *didn't* have, no matter how much money she socked away. He had a name that held weight, and he had connections.

The very things he'd hoped to leave behind him were precisely what he could use to help her.

EVANGELINE TAPPED HER FOOT. Augustus released a series of confused sounds as his head flew back off the desk.

"I think it says more about you than me, that I knew you'd be here in the office on a Saturday."

"Saturday," Augustus repeated. He hastily wiped at the corners of his mouth.

"Yes, Augustus, the day following Friday. You didn't go home last night. Probably confused the hell out of your little pet."

"My pet?"

"You're tired, not stupid."

Ekatherina. In a quick panic, he pictured her the night before, awaiting him to walk her out. Possibly wondering if she should bother him, or if he was somehow cross with her. His heart sank.

"You haven't stayed the night here since before the place opened," Evangeline said. "I think I know why. Can I guess?"

"Seems like you're about to anyway," Augustus grumbled.

She grinned. "Bingo. I am. You needed an excuse for why you weren't at the party today."

Augustus glanced up at the clock with shock. It was nearly three in the afternoon. Had he slept that long? How?

"The party." He searched his groggy brain. "You're going to need to help me out here."

"Rory and Carolina's party, you oaf!" She leaned over his desk and fell forward on her palms. "Don't play coy, Aggie. Everyone noted your absence, and they all know why you didn't come."

"And why is that, Evangeline? Other than the fact I wouldn't have come even if I remembered it?"

"If you wanted people to think you don't care, showing up and acting gracious and supportive would have sent that message more clearly."

"But I *don't* care," he snapped. "I'm happy for the two of them. That thing with Carolina only happened once, and I put a stop to it for a reason."

"She was good for you. She could have been so good for you, you know?"

"Thanks for your confidence in me to handle my life without a woman," Augustus gruffed. "And that's a good reason to be with someone, you think? That they'd be good for you?"

"Happiness isn't a disease, you know."

"Adding *you know* to the end of your sentences doesn't remove the condescension, *you know*, or make you sound any more wise."

Evangeline pulled herself up and crossed her arms. "It's summer. The birds are singing. Love is in the air."

"You're a woman of science. You know love isn't in the goddamn air."

Evangeline wrinkled her lips and made a derisive sound. "Colin and Catherine are marrying soon. Your brother's engagement party is right around the corner. You could at least *pretend* to give a shit about any of this."

"Catherine is in love with that very same brother of ours, who is marrying a woman who is more miserable than all of us combined. And Rory and Carolina? Are we to pretend that Rory didn't marry Carolina to get back at Colleen? How are these things worthy of celebration?"

"What is *wrong* with you?" Evangeline demanded. "You're even more cranky than usual."

The venom died in Augustus. He leaned back in his chair and closed his eyes for a moment. "I didn't mean to fall asleep here. It was an accident. One that had nothing to do with the party."

"Oh?" Evangeline slipped into the chair across from him. "Any time you do something that's not like you, I assume this deviation implies a disruption in your life."

Augustus rolled his eyes.

"It's that girl, isn't it?"

"If you're talking about who I assume you're talking about, she has a name."

"Ekatherina." Evangeline made a sour face. "Carolina was good for you. Ekatherina is not."

"My interest in Ekatherina is not romantic."

"But you *are* interested in her."

Augustus had a flash of guilt as he thought about the envelope locked in the top drawer of his desk. "I find her plight intriguing."

"What a bunch of bullshit. Her plight is intriguing?"

"Evie, how many young women do you know who found a way to escape a complicated life? Who came to another country, learning a language not native to them, and worked night and day to make a better life?"

Evangeline softened. "Sure, she's a hard worker. And I don't know what it would be like to grow up amongst all those commie infidels, waiting hours for bread, getting arrested for questioning your government. But there's something not right about that girl, Augustus—"

"Ekatherina."

"*Ekatherina*. Fine. She's done a lot for herself, I'll give her that. She's resilient. But resilient people aren't often the ones most concerned with lawfulness. She's very determined. Determined people find ways around the rules, not through them."

"That's very nihilistic, Evangeline, even for you."

Evangeline slouched in her chair. She watched him. "You really *don't* care about Carolina, do you?"

"I said I didn't." He quickly added, "I'm happy she's happy."

"She would have been happier with you."

Augustus laughed. "Come on, even you know that's not true. I would have made her miserable. I don't think there's a woman alive who could live with me."

"Except Ekatherina."

"We're back to that, are we?"

"You can deny things all you want, but you forget I know you."

"Then you should know I'm really tired of talking about this with you." Augustus pulled himself out of his chair. His body ached, head to toe, from the cramped sleep his chair had provided. "And you know, Evangeline, I'd think you of all people would recognize the passion for learning in Ekatherina. She's hungry for knowledge. You should relate to that."

"Don't take financial advice from her."

"What?"

"She told me she's offering you advice on your investments."

He shook his head. "Really? I know how to invest my money. You know that. I listen to her advice because it makes her happy when I do. It just so happens most of what she suggests to me is exactly what Jamie Sullivan has already recommended. If she thinks the advice came from her alone, what's the harm in it?"

"There you go, trying to make her happy."

"Are you done now?"

"Never," she said and laughed. "But since you're awake now, let's go check out that townhouse on Esplanade Mom is interested in."

Augustus nodded. He reached for his briefcase, but then decided better of it. Maybe this was a good weekend, for once, not to work. He'd promised his mother his help and had put her off, but he shouldn't put that off any longer.

"Oh, I almost forgot," Evangeline said, as she pressed the down arrow on their newly-installed elevator. "I won't be leaving for Massachusetts next month."

He turned to her. "What? Why?"

"Let's just say Colleen is about to share some news of her own, and I think I can wait another year."

SEVEN
FRIEND OF A FRIEND

Scotland.

It wasn't that Colleen's interest hadn't been in earnest when she applied to University of Edinburgh's medical program. Even the edges of this idea filled her with a very unexpected thrill, in a way few things in her life ever had.

And had she thought they'd reject her and just thwart the dream before she could up and leave? No, she'd known her grades and transcripts were solid enough. She knew she'd be asked to interview, and that when they called, she'd ace that, too. Her admissions packet had been top of the line.

Yet it had still felt hazy and surreal, like the strange caprices of a growing child. Nothing more than a fantastical idea. Her world was here, with her family. With her deep, abiding love for caring for them, and for the history that built them.

Now, though, she had the letter in her hand, confirming her acceptance into one of the best medical programs in Europe. In Edinburgh, where she'd never been but longed to go.

The program started in the fall, next year. She had a full year, then, to make her plans here at home before departing not only the family home, but the city, the state, and the entire country.

Colleen finished Professor Green's stack of tests an hour ago. Though she wasn't taking summer courses this term, being as far ahead as she was, she'd offered to come help him, and he hadn't hesitated to accept that offer. She wouldn't have any courses with him in her final year of college at Tulane, and her disappointment in that was surprising; not the fact of it, but the depth.

The door opened and Professor Green's familiar gait sounded across the floor.

"My afternoon class was cancelled," he announced. "Someone pulled the fire bell on the other side of campus and now they want to clear the whole damn campus." He shook his head as he assembled his folders, sliding them into the leather folds of his briefcase.

"The whole campus? But why?"

"This political climate," he replied, as if that should be obvious. Colleen made a mental note. "Did you know we had two bomb threats? This week, I mean. This week alone!"

Colleen's mouth dropped. "But there's been no news about that."

"We don't advertise the behavior of bad actors. Besides, we didn't want to rile up the students over nothing. I shouldn't even have told you, but I know you can keep a secret."

Colleen flushed. "I would never repeat anything you said to me in confidence."

Professor Green secured the buckle and looked up with a smile. "I know that. That's why I told you. I trust you." His eyes lingered on her a moment longer, and then he snapped back into action. "They're almost done clearing campus. You'll need to leave, too. You didn't hear the bell?"

She shook her head.

He squinted behind his glasses as he looked around the room.

"Ahh, yes. They haven't outfitted this building with the inside alarms yet. I'll send a note to facilities." He turned back to her. "Come have lunch with me, Colleen. Now, I know you've probably got your slew of excuses loaded, but there's nothing wrong with two adults enjoying each other's company."

Colleen had assessed and reassessed his previous invite so many times she'd made herself dizzy with her assumptions. Professor Green was married, but he didn't wear a ring, and she'd seen no evidence of a family in pictures on his desk, or in his office. But this combination of facts could mean anything, and, aside from him being her elder, professionally and otherwise, she wasn't comfortable not understanding his personal situation.

Then again, she was probably overthinking the whole thing, which was a particular specialty of hers. What interest could he possibly have in her?

"Your mind is whirring. I can see it," he teased. His smile lit up his whole face, and his blue eyes sparkled behind his thick glasses. "Maybe I can help. Yes, I'm legally married, Colleen, but we've lived separately for years. We'll eventually work things out with the lawyer, but for now, it's financially easier for us to just live the way we have been."

Had he seen her staring at his ring finger?

"At least, I *assume* that's your hesitation?"

"It's one of them," Colleen replied. "I also don't want to get you in any kind of trouble here at the school."

He grinned from one side of his mouth. "I'm not trying to get you into bed, you know."

Her stomach lit up with a mess of flutters. "No! No, I know. I know that."

"I see you more as a colleague, Colleen. You're not on the level of the other kids coming and going to classes. You're ahead of your time. I'd say you're going places, but I think you're already halfway there."

"I'm leaving for Scotland next fall," she blurted.

He nodded slowly. "I assumed as much when they asked for my recommendation."

"They asked you?"

"They did. And I not only gave one by phone, I wrote a letter singing your praises."

"You'd do that for me?" Colleen exhaled and steadied herself in her chair. "You did that?"

"I would, I did, and I'd do it again," he said. "You're going to go on from here to do amazing things. And I'll be able to say I was but a small part of it."

Colleen blushed deeper. "Stop. You've helped me in so many ways. You have no idea."

"So tell me," he pressed, still smiling. "Over lunch. Or drinks, if that suits your fancy."

Colleen was abashed with how easily she was about to acquiesce. The invitation was innocuous enough, but the underlying situation was far more complicated... though tempting.

But she couldn't, for other reasons. "Another time. Really," she added, when his face fell. "I actually have a date tonight."

He gave her an appraising nod. "A date, huh? Anyone I know?"

"Friend of a friend." This was a half-truth. Rory wasn't really her friend anymore, as much as she tried. But accepting the blind date offer that he'd proposed served two purposes as she saw it. One, it would show Rory she'd moved on, regardless of whether that was ultimately true, and two, it would show she was capable of the same level of normalcy as her peers.

"I see. Well, I won't keep you, but don't let the guards catch you in here." He winked. "I appreciate your help this summer, Colleen. You've really been a godsend."

She smiled and looked down at her hands, wound in her lap. "I'll help you as long as you'll have me."

"Don't make promises you can't keep," he said, his tone that of a tease, his eyes something else entirely.

BOBBY HAD HARDLY PAUSED for breath in the past twenty minutes, as he regaled Colleen with nostalgic anecdotes from his glorious, but short-lived, high school football career. Colleen knew next to nothing about football, or any sport, but she knew enough to know that the role of a tackle was not as prestigious as he'd like her to believe.

"And then Joe, you know Joe, one of *those* quarterbacks, couldn't help himself. I used to tell him to just *think* for a half second before putting the ball in play, but he couldn't handle the pressure of the defensive line and always had to get rid of the damn thing. Damn, damn fine quarterback, if not for that. But good guards and tackles know the weaknesses of their quarterback and know how to hold off the line. Conrad shouldn't have caught that damn ball, everyone knew it, but we held off defense and that's why we won state."

"How nice," Colleen remarked. Somewhere, Rory was laughing to himself, imagining the blind date going down probably exactly like this.

"When Joe didn't get the scholarship, he trashed the locker room. Pulled a whole row of lockers off the wall like a Neanderthal!" Bobby shook his head. He drained the last of his beer and slid the mug to the edge of the table, awaiting his third. "I could have told him, scouts are watching him lose his cool. He can't get credit for half the touchdown passes, not when the running backs had to be circus performers to get that ball across the end zone."

"What else do you like to do?"

"What do you mean?"

"You've been in college a few years now."

Bobby blinked without responding. She couldn't read his expression, but he offered a small nod.

"Rory said you go to LSU New Orleans?"

"I was hoping for Baton Rouge, for the football," Bobby said. He'd started to shift in his seat, sliding up and down over the wood, crossing and uncrossing his arms. "There was a mix-up in the paperwork."

Colleen had rarely seen a stronger case of denial than this one, but she wasn't going to be the one to tell him his dream hadn't died because of a problem with paperwork. "So what else do you do? Do you play any other sports? Are you part of any clubs?"

Bobby's face lit up. "I party with the St. Charles Polo Club every Wednesday, Friday, and Saturday. They close the place down after seven, and then that baby is all ours. We're still going strong long after all the bars in the French Quarter are closed. Wanna come sometime?"

"I don't really party," Colleen replied, and though she'd never been ashamed of this fact, she felt suddenly like she was twice Bobby's age and half as interesting.

Colleen sighed before she could stop herself, but Bobby was still rambling on about all the blueblood kids and their ragers.

What was Rory's angle here? Revenge? Trying to show her how good she'd had it with him? There was no way he'd thought Colleen would have anything at all in common with this oaf, and maybe that was the point. Or maybe there was no point, and Colleen was thinking too far into it. But Bobby didn't make Colleen miss Rory... instead, being around this man, who was likely a fair representation of many of the college-age boys available to date, only served to alienate her further. She wasn't a part of this world. She'd never belonged to it, not even as a child, and every step she'd taken carried her further toward the future she wanted. She was okay with being an old woman at the age of twenty-one, because that's where she was happy and safe, and what was wrong with that? Bobby was no more connecting with her than she was him, though he would probably be less bothered by it. When Colleen spent her time on something—or someone—it was an investment, not a lark.

"We're not digging on anything hard. Some booze, maybe some grass sometimes. Every now and then someone shows up with some acid, but only the good stuff. No one wants a bad trip. And we have a strictly no powder rule, because our parents have connections but not *those* connections, if you know what I'm saying." He rambled on, oblivious to the idea she might not want to do any of those things.

"What are you going to school for?" she asked, when he took a breath.

"Uh... well, I'm between majors."

"Which majors are you between?"

He grinned and ran his hand through his long black hair. "All of them?"

"What do you enjoy doing?"

Bobby frowned. "You asked that before."

"And you never really answered."

He shrugged. "Football is really all I care about. But unless they get my paperwork straightened out, that's not happening."

Colleen nodded through her struggle to connect with anything this young man was saying. What she knew about him going into the date, that he was the son of a small-time politician, seemed to explain most of what she was hearing now. He had all the markings of someone who, in the absence of accountability, had chosen to meander through life, knowing that any failure to launch would not be a failure to land on his feet.

He reminded her of Charles, except that Charles had more depth of character. Charles was an asshole who would never see consequences for any of his ill-advised behavior, but he commanded a room.

And as Bobby returned to the subjects he was comfortable with, football and passing a good time, Colleen's own thoughts wandered to a certain man with the horn-rimmed glasses and patches on his Houndstooth coat. The always-thoughtful look in his eyes; how he saw through to her, to the woman she'd worked so hard to become. Everyone else gave Colleen a hard time for these things, but Professor Green understood. She imagined he'd been the same way when he was a young man, trying to navigate a silly world through serious eyes.

It would be unwise to accept his invitation... if there was ever fire for someone as reserved as Colleen to play with, it would be this. How many stories of teacher-student romances ever ended well for either party? Of course, Maureen's experience was an extreme example, but even among adults, such things were taboo and destined for disaster. And yes, she was jumping ahead, assuming drinks would lead to more, but Colleen's mind wasn't capable of living in the moment only. She had to consider all possible outcomes, and though she struggled to understand his interest in her, a relationship *was* a possible outcome of accepting his offer.

Was there any outcome that didn't lead to her misery?

All outcomes came to one natural termination point, though: Scotland. Even if they defied the odds and fell in love, she was leaving. She needed to leave. To grow for her family, she had to first grow for herself, and she couldn't do that here in New Orleans, stifled by all the baggage of being a Deschanel.

"Wanna get out of here?" Bobby asked.

Yes, but not with you.

EIGHT
FOR THE SAKE OF ALL

The day wasn't supposed to be windy. Only when a tropical storm, or a full-fledged hurricane, was on the horizon did the wind really pick up in the summer, and by all accounts, Colin and Catherine had chosen a beautiful weekend to be married.

Charles had to cover his cigarette with his free hand as he took a drag. The breeze passed through the dozen or so oaks standing sentry over the small row of cabins, and the sound competed with the cicadas, which weren't so much singing as screaming today. The day was sweltering, but their retreat was shaded by the ancient trees, and because of this he hadn't even broken a sweat yet.

The groomsmen and groom stayed in one cabin, and the bridesmaids and bride in another. Colin had chosen his two brothers, Rory and Patrick, to stand with Charles, the best man. Charles had never liked Rory, though even he could admit the reason had more to do with him fooling about with Colleen than anything else. Patrick, a year younger than Rory, had been annoying as a kid and wasn't much better as a new adult. But these would be his cabin-mates for the weekend, until they all scattered back to their lives in New Orleans, leaving the newlyweds to their business.

Catherine's maid of honor was supposed to be her roommate, but they'd had a falling out and now Carolina was standing in. The bridesmaids were Colin's sister, Chelsea, still in high school, and a Sullivan cousin, Olivia, who none of them knew especially well.

Charles didn't have the presence of mind to be sad at the motley crew making up the bridal party. He was too deeply hurt to think very far into how neither Colin nor Catherine had people in their lives outside their families who could celebrate this day with them. That though Charles was Colin's best friend, he'd never lived up to the title as much as Colin had for him, and while he'd die for Colin if the situation presented itself, that situation never had, so he remained the one who benefitted the most from their arrangement.

He'd never been to The Myrtles before now. The plantation was less than two hours from Ophélie, just north of Baton Rouge, but he'd never had occasion to make his way up. Nor a reason, not when he lived on the most prominent plantation on River Road already, and was surrounded by many others. When he thought of getting out and seeing new things, other plantations were pretty damn low on the list.

Charles had heard The Myrtles was haunted, but he didn't believe in that stuff, though he didn't doubt what Maureen claimed to be experiencing with all their dead relatives. But Maureen was special. The average person was not. Ghosts were for people with overactive imaginations and nothing better to do.

Still... the Spanish moss pouring down from the branches like macabre waterfalls... the dark pall cast over the land despite the sun beaming overhead... there was something to it all. Something.

The men and women weren't supposed to interact for the

two days leading up to the wedding ceremony. Really, it was Catherine who cared that much about tradition, and everyone else—except Colin, who dared not upset his bride-to-be—wandered the grounds without worrying about tradition. Catherine and Colin hadn't come out of the cabins at all, and Charles was surprised to find how superstitious they both were about something so ridiculous. Their marriage was more likely to be doomed by Catherine not loving her husband than it was by them accidentally catching a glimpse of one another.

There were more than two cabins on the property, but Catherine's family couldn't afford to buy out the others for three days. Charles, secretly, rented the others out himself, and everyone talked about how lucky they were that no one was staying in the empty ones.

Even after everything, he still loved her. He still couldn't bear to see her unhappy.

"You all ready for tomorrow?" Rory asked this, as though Charles had any job at all other than standing by Colin's side and trying not to look miserable.

"Haven't quite nailed my juggling routine, but the clown suit arrived this morning."

Rory watched him, blinking, as if deciding whether Charles was serious or not.

"How's your elopement working out for you?"

Rory leaned into the post holding up the porch awning. "It's great. Carolina and I are really happy."

"Still fantasizing about Colleen?"

"Charles, come on."

"You know she's leaving for Scotland next fall?"

Rory's face revealed the answer. "That's good. It will be really good for her."

"Right." Charles laughed, took one last drag, and stubbed his cigarette across the bottom of his shoe. He flicked the butt into the grass.

Rory looked around before leaning in. "What about you? Still lusting after your best friend's fiancée?"

"She wasn't his fiancée when she came to my bed."

"I never told anyone, you know. Not even Carolina."

"I fucking know you didn't," Charles said. "Or we wouldn't be sitting here, the day before their wedding."

"I hope you're over it now," Rory said. "For the sake of everyone involved."

"Cat is the one you should be worried about." Charles stood. He spread his knuckles, enjoying the loud pops as he cracked them, and walked away.

The women all had activities planned leading up to the wedding day, but the men were far less organized. Charles realized at one point he was supposed to be the one responsible for coordinating the groomsmen, but he possessed neither the desire nor the knowledge to do much. Instead, he'd sent out for two cases of beer and had Richard drive up a stack of films to watch. But he'd been the only one to touch the beer—he'd forgotten, the Sullivans were a bunch of failed Irishman teetotalers—and no one wanted to be indoors watching films when the world outside was so much more interesting.

So the men wandered the property, separate and aimless, while the women stayed together, doing crafting projects, team building games, and other things that were so completely foreign to Charles.

He had no interest in hanging out with the Sullivan men, so he made his way off the grounds and followed the road toward the river. The Mississippi was a staple in his life; a constant, whether he was at Ophélie or in New Orleans, and it was both a beacon and an anchor. He'd kept his angst hidden from the group, but he knew he couldn't carry what he was feeling into the next day. He hated them both, hated them with all his heart, but he loved them, and he would smile through the worst day of his life and do his duty.

"Huck!"

Charles froze at the sweet sound. He didn't turn. A car flew by on the road and the wind blew him back.

Catherine came around him, approaching with a slow, tentative gait. "What are you doing all the way out here?"

"Why are you following me?" He looked past her. "Where are your girls?"

"We're all taking naps. Beauty rest and all that." She smiled so bright he wanted to throw up from the pain.

You don't need beauty rest. You're perfect. Ahh, the things he would have said to her, once upon a time. They weren't lines with Cat; every word had been an authentic extension of his heart, each one surprising him with how much closer they brought him to the man he wished to be.

"If anyone sees you with me, it's not gonna be good," he said.

"I know," she said. She twisted her heel in the gravel. "I need to see you, though. Tonight, meet me behind the old cistern on the other side of the property. Midnight. The witching hour." She said the last with a hesitant giggle.

"Why should I?"

"You're here, aren't you?"

"For Colin. I'm here for Colin."

"Okay, then. Because you love me. And it's the last thing I'll ever ask of you."

She flashed one more smile, this one fleeting and anxious, and darted back off the way she'd come.

CHARLES WASN'T sure she'd follow through. Catherine had floated in and out of his life with her indecision, and he wasn't surprised she'd want to see him the night before she made the biggest commitment of her life. But this same wearying trait of hers, guessing which way her wind was blowing, made him doubt the odds of seeing her face appear in the moonlight.

"I didn't think you'd come," her soft voice said from behind him.

Charles laughed. "You knew I'd come, Cat."

"Maybe," she cooed. She took on the pliant persona of bedroom Catherine, ready to please.

Catherine wrapped her fingers over the top of his muscled arm. "Colin doesn't know how hard tomorrow will be. He can never know."

"Your wedding day isn't supposed to be hard." Charles nudged them further behind the cistern, to block all cabin views. He brushed her hand away.

"Not everyone marries for love."

"You're not living in some third world banana republic!" Charles cried out. "Arranged marriages don't happen anymore."

"Oh really? Cordelia?"

"You *chose* Colin," Charles charged, ignoring her dig. He was doing what he had to do for his family. She was doing this for reasons that made sense to no one, probably least of all herself. "And long before I was engaged to Cordelia, so don't go trying that on for size, either. I have my reasons for agreeing to marry her, but you *damn well fucking know* I would have married you in an instant! Without even a moment's hesitation!"

"There would have been no advantage to marrying me. Your mother wouldn't have allowed it, and no matter what you say, I know what she thinks matters to you," Cat said. She leaned into the rusted metal and closed her eyes. "You can only say these things to me now, when we're both unavailable."

"You'll never know now, huh?" Charles wanted to light up, but the smoke would draw attention to their rendezvous. "And speaking of unavailable, you picked a hell of a time to have this conversation."

"Better now than after I'm Mrs. Sullivan," she said. Her eyes were still closed. Her skin was soft porcelain in the light of the full moon. "I've spent all my life wondering if I was on the right path. I question *everything* I do, Huck. Everything. I think and then overthink, until I can't see the forest for the trees anymore. I don't come from much, and I told myself I didn't need much, but do you know how much we moved around as kids? Do you know why I didn't have someone already in mind to be my maid of honor? Most women have to choose. I had a roommate who I only half-liked."

Charles said nothing.

"I don't have friends, Huck! My friends are Colin's friends, and he doesn't have many either, except you, and... well, I don't need to say why *that's* complicated, do I? There's this thing I do... I've never told anyone this... my parents don't even know. We used to move so often that I couldn't sleep at night for all the anxiety. Wondering where I'd be sleeping the following night, and if we'd go hungry at dinner, as we often did. I needed something that was mine, that I could hold on to. You see, I found this old cooler at the lake that someone had abandoned, and I took it home and I cleaned it up. Scrubbed it with bleach until it was like new, except half the color was gone, but that was okay. And then I started sneaking food from the kitchen and putting it in my cooler. Because I was afraid that one day we'd have to leave again, and this time we'd go somewhere worse. And you know what? I still have that cooler, and I still keep it filled."

"Cat..." Charles shoved his hands deep into the pockets of his heavy denim. "Stability isn't happiness."

"You can only say that because you've always had it," Catherine said. The pale light glinted off the tears sliding down her cheeks. "I will always know where I stand with Colin. With you, every day is new, and that scares me. You don't know anything, Huck. You have everything, but you know nothing. And I don't care what you know, because I love you anyway. I love you even when I shouldn't."

Charles was weak in the knees at the unexpected arrival of these words. The second time she'd said them, and both times now she'd been in distress when the words slipped out. They didn't hurt any less. "You've made the choice that you can live with." He'd never chosen his words more carefully. "And yet, you're standing here with me, in the middle of the night, hours before you're going to be another man's wife. I need you to tell me why."

"I just did!" Catherine sobbed. She buried her face in her palms. Her small frame shook, and it took everything in him not to go to her, to fold her into his arms. "I love you, Charles! I love you, and if you said it back, if you told me you loved me, too, I'd throw away all this safety for love."

Charles exhaled into the cool night. He thought he'd be weaker... that he'd even enjoy being right. All along, she'd loved Colin for his steadfast safety, a Sullivan trait if there ever was one, and her heart fought for something more. Here's where he should tell her that he could offer her stability as well. There wasn't anything money couldn't buy, nothing she needed he couldn't provide. Every day didn't have to be new. It didn't have to be anything she didn't want or need.

But she hadn't come to him with a cool head and a level heart. And Charles had the rare presence of mind to imagine her seeking out Colin on her wedding day to Charles, turning to the same indecision and irrationality her parents had taught her in their nomadic lifestyle.

"I do love you. I've never loved anyone else, and I can't see myself loving anyone else again. I'm not made for love the way other men are, and I can live with that." Releasing the words came with the relinquishment of a tremendous burden. "But you can't look to me to make this decision for you. Whether you marry Colin or not should have nothing to do with me, and I can't tell you what to do, Catherine. I can't do this for you. I won't."

Charles let himself look at her, take her all the way in, one last time before he shuffled off into the night.

CHARLES SHOWED up to the wedding off his gourd. He'd taken eight bumps of coke, two more than usual, and even that didn't dull the ache in his chest, and the regret forming a hard lump in his belly.

The morning after, when he awoke in his own bed, he mercifully remembered almost nothing at all from the ceremony or the reception.

What he did remember came in brief, chaotic flashes.

The length of Catherine's train that seemed to stretch all the way to the river.

Colin's father breaking down into tears of joy.

Chelsea sneaking a flask out of her bosom when she thought no one was looking.

Patrick's long sigh, followed by, under his breath, "She's a stunner. How did Colin... of all people..."

For better or worse. Richer or poorer. I now pronounce you man and wife.

Olivia, the cousin, sitting on Charles' lap in the horse barn, bouncing away with her frilly dress hitched up over her waist. His first Sullivan conquest, though he suspected Chelsea would find her way to him sooner or later.

Sleeping it all off in the backseat as Colleen and Augustus drove him home in silence.

Home. Where he was the master. Where emotion, and love, and pain couldn't touch him.

NINE
ONLY LUNCH

Colleen raced to Magnolia Grace, coming so close to breaking the speed limit that this near-rebellion only made her heart beat harder and faster.

She angled the car against the curb on Prytania and slammed forward as she braked too hard. She was halfway to the front door when she realized she'd left her purse in the front seat, and even in the Garden District, even in her state of mind, that was too big of a risk.

Evangeline stepped out onto the porch. Her hand came up to shield her eyes from the midday sun, which today was too hot, too bright, even for New Orleans.

Her body language shifted as she watched Colleen race down the path toward the wide steps.

"Colleen, what is it? Is it Mama?"

Colleen shook her head and took Evangeline by the arm as she led her inside. "No, nothing so serious. I didn't mean to scare you, but for once, I'm the one who's desperate for some advice."

"You? I'm intrigued!" Evangeline's worried lines dissolved from her face, replaced by a wide grin.

"You won't be smiling when I tell you the trouble I've gotten myself into."

Evangeline stopped just inside the front door. "Real trouble, or your idea of trouble, which would be speeding tickets as mortal sins?"

"This is bigger than that." Colleen looked around. "Augustus is at the office, right?"

Evangeline snickered. "Where else would he be? If you want to catch him at home, try between one and three in the morning."

"Okay." Colleen pulled at the bun sitting at the nape of her neck. She spun around with her eyes closed. "Okay, okay."

"Jesus," Evangeline said. "You *are* in a state."

"Do you remember me telling you about Professor Green?"

Evangeline's mouth parted, and her eyes widened. "Let's go sit down for this."

"Don't look at me like that!"

Evangeline pulled her lips back together into a tight line. "I remember you talking about Philip."

"I've never called him that, don't be catty."

Evangeline sat on the couch, and Colleen joined her after a pause.

"Okay, so your professor. You just got back from shagging him in his office, I take it?"

"Evangeline! I said I needed advice, not your attitude. No, I didn't *shag* him."

"Then I don't know why you look like you need a lawyer."

"I do not."

"So, what? If you didn't screw, then what?"

"Well..." Colleen tried to sit back, to nestle in and get comfortable, but she was too stiff. She ran her hands over her green slacks and inhaled a deep breath. "He's very nice. Most of the teachers I've had in college look at students a certain way. Like they're just children, or less than. Not worth their time.

They look past you, not at you. And even if they like you, once you're out of sight, you're out of mind. But not Professor Green. He looks me right in the eyes when he speaks to me, and he doesn't go somewhere else in his mind when I'm talking. He seems to be *genuinely* interested in what I'm saying. In who I am, and what matters to me as well. I didn't notice it at first, because I figured this special treatment was thanks for grading his papers and making his life easier. I'm very efficient, you know. But I realized at the start of summer that it was more than polite interest."

"You seem surprised that this guy is into you," Evangeline said.

Colleen thought for a moment before answering. "That's not an indictment of me, but rather the system. I'm just a student. But he seems to have seen something more in me, and we're past the point of convincing myself I'm just imagining it."

"So something did happen then?"

"Not what you think, but yes... and I could have prevented it, but I didn't, and that's why I need advice. You know me. You know my values... my moral code. My willpower isn't easily compromised."

"No," Evangeline agreed. "You're goddamn Mother Theresa, relatively speaking. You know, if Mother Theresa was a Deschanel and slightly fucked up."

"I'm sure you committed blasphemy somewhere in there," Colleen said with a sigh.

"Okay, I need to ask you something first. You need to be honest with me."

"You don't have to say that. Of course I'll be honest."

Evangeline nodded. "This all doesn't have something to do with Rory and his shotgun wedding to Carolina, does it?"

Colleen didn't tense at the mention of this, as she once had, not very long ago. "No, and if I'm being perfectly honest, meeting a man like Philip has helped me to see that what Rory and I had wasn't lasting. It wasn't enough for me, and I was holding onto a childhood romance out of nostalgia."

"Philip." Evangeline smirked. "Now I feel like we're getting somewhere."

"I never called him that until today."

"About today, then. Wanna start at the beginning? Or skip to the good stuff?"

Colleen waved her hand in the air, pretending to smack her. "I used to study in his office, because I had a key and it was quiet, but I started to think perhaps I was giving him the wrong idea. So I've taken to studying in the cafeteria. Even though it's loud, it's the noise of people who have nothing to do with me, so I'm not distracted like I am at home.

"He came in, and I pretended not to see him. You see, I didn't want to give him the wrong idea about spending all that time in his office, but I *also* didn't want him to think I was avoiding him."

"Oh, tangled web!" Evangeline cried in delight.

"You're enjoying this far too much."

"If I am?"

"Anyway, he saw me. We made small talk, and then he asked if I'd had lunch. By this time he'd been talking to me almost five minutes, which was enough to start to draw attention to us. I told him I hadn't, he asked me to have lunch with him, and I started to say no, but... God, as my witness, Evangeline, I swear it wasn't me who said yes. I said no in my head, but yes is what came out."

"Maybe you *are* a human, after all."

Colleen swatted the air again. "People were looking at this point, so I said, I'll meet you there. He was amused by this, which made me feel like a child, because if he wasn't concerned, why should I be? But I was, and so I said, we need to leave the area. He suggested Carrollton, but I don't quite think he was getting what I meant, so I told him Metairie instead. I don't know how he came up with a suggestion so quick, but without hesitation he said to meet him at Salvaggio's, which he said was a quiet little Sicilian restaurant near Metairie Cemetery, just behind the New Orleans Country Club. I was just working up the nerve to correct my answer to no, when he winked and left. I couldn't exactly run after him without making the audience situation worse, so I returned to my studies for a few more minutes."

"So you had no choice."

"I detect sarcasm, Evangeline, but no, I didn't feel it would be good form to not show up, seeing as I had no way to reach him to let him know I'd changed my mind. Nor did I have time to point out that Metairie Cemetery and the New Orleans Country Club are actually within New Orleans city limits, and not in Metairie."

"So you went to Salvatore's..."

"Salvaggio's."

"Salvaggio's. And then?"

COLLEEN DROVE around the block twice before she spotted the restaurant. It was easy to miss, a small brick building nursed behind two large buildings. The parking lot was almost empty, and the four arched windows were blacked out, giving it the air of a place forgotten. If she hadn't spotted Professor Green's Volvo parked to the side, she wouldn't have exited her car.

The inside was as empty as the parking lot, but the colorful décor eased her mind. An older couple sat under a brick arch that was wrapped in faux olive branches, and a businessman ate alone, reading the newspaper.

Professor Green sat alone in a corner, looking oddly out of sorts. She was so used to seeing him commanding an audience in the dark lecture hall, or poring over his syllabus and notes in preparation. He was an unusual, almost painfully assured man, but at present he looked like an apprehensive teenager.

He didn't think she would show, Colleen realized. He wasn't

nervous to be around her, he was anxious he'd played his hand and lost. If Evangeline were here, she'd have all sorts of insights into the professor's body language, choice of seat, choice of restaurant. Evangeline was a walking tome of interesting but ultimately useless information in social settings; a veritable mix of *Gray's Anatomy* and Freud's *Psychopathology of Everyday Life.* She would analyze his decision to wait without something to do or read; why he sat instead of waiting for Colleen in the parking lot.

And as she imagined Evangeline's assessment of such things, Colleen became aware she was doing it, too.

It's only lunch, he'd said, but they'd both understood, without words, without anything other than the strange energies that exist between humans, that this was more.

She could have read his mind, but two things prevented her. Firstly, this crossed her own self-imposed ethical boundary, where she'd promised to herself, and to the unknowing world around her, that she'd never employ this unless she believed herself or someone else to be in danger. Colleen so seldom read minds anymore that she was no longer very good at sifting through the randomness for anything useful. This realization was both maddening and also a relief.

Secondly, and she only knew this because she had broken her one rule, but only for a second, just as he'd asked her to lunch: Professor Green was either a most unusual man, whose mind was closed off to the telepaths of the world, or he himself was blocking.

Tante Ophelia once said that there was no such thing as a mind that couldn't be read, so long as the host wasn't aware to stop it. If her great-aunt, who'd lived close to a hundred years, whose father and grandfather had lived through the Civil War, believed this to be true, who was Colleen to question it?

If Philip Green was blocking, where had he learned it, and

why would he know to do it around her? Blocking took tremendous energy, too much to continue the effort endlessly, so if he was blocking, then it was happening selectively.

If he was blocking, then he had a specific reason. What could it mean? And how could she ask without outing herself?

Professor Green noticed her shuffling through her mental conspiracy theories, smiled broadly, and waved from his table. Colleen returned the smile and made her way over, now sufficiently even more nervous about agreeing than she had been sitting amongst hundreds of students in the cafeteria.

"You made it," he said, with a light note of surprise.

"The place wasn't easy to find," Colleen said. She let him pull her chair out and ease her back in, even though this felt more and more like a date every minute.

Professor Green chuckled. "I'm sorry. I should have mentioned that, but I was in a hurry to leave."

"I noticed."

"I could already see you working through your very calculated and reasonable list of refusals."

"Was it that obvious?" Colleen, without consciously realizing it, reached for her cloth napkin and settled it into her lap. Her hands went to work on the hard cotton, a way of keeping at least part of herself busy and centered.

He laughed again, a bright, sparkling sound that matched his brilliant eyes. "What would you like to hear? That you're the master of misdirection? The authority on avoidance? The expert in evasion?"

"Your alliteration is quite impressive for a science teacher."

"When one commits themselves to scholarly endeavors, one must commit to them all."

"Do you also espouse terrible puns? Someone might *commit* you for that."

"My, wouldn't that be a dramatic way to show one's

jealousy."

Colleen regarded him very seriously, and he in return, and then they both erupted in laughter that broke the surface of the ice formed around the witty returns to keep things on the level.

"Professor Green—"

"Philip."

"I can't call you that," Colleen said before he'd even finished the second half of his name. "I'm your student."

His smile faded some. "You're not my student anymore."

And what would Evangeline have to say to *that*?

"You're not a child, Colleen. And you're more than a student. I teach many, many young men and women each year, and I remember some of them years later. The ones who took the lessons seriously and made time after the lecture to engage me further. Those are the students who went somewhere, I'm certain of that. I know where several of them landed, and I may have played a part in that."

Colleen's heart sank a little at the insinuation she wasn't the first, or the only, student he'd written a letter for, and she felt ridiculous for this disappointment, because his recommendations were a part of his job.

"I won't tell you how long I've been doing this, because it will reveal I'm not the young, svelte man I know you believe me to be." He grinned, but she didn't miss the hopeful gleam. "My biography is out there, in several publications, if you're so inclined. But I don't think you care how old I am."

"No, I don't," Colleen said. "Age is either a number that holds us back or pushes us forward."

"Of course you'd say that," he said. "I'm never surprised with you, but I'm always amazed. I enjoy not knowing where I stand with you. I don't even mind the disadvantage, or the vulnerability. Many men are afraid to be vulnerable, but I don't think you can face the idea of your own strength without first understanding how to be exposed to another, for their review and assessment."

Colleen prayed she wasn't wearing the heat building within her on her face as well.

She thanked the waitress who brought them water. She started to order a glass of cabernet, when Professor Green—Philip, he had insisted—instead ordered a bottle of what he said was his favorite Sangiovese from Tuscany. He then said they'd share a plate of carbonara, assuring Colleen with a laugh that neither of them could finish a plate themselves.

"I spent a semester studying in Florence, when I thought I had a call to be an art major." They both laughed. "Ask me about the Renaissance and prepare to be dazzled."

Colleen had very little interest in art, but she'd always been drawn to the dark, rich colors of the Italian Renaissance... of the strange mix of beauty and finance that lay over the history of Florence. In her less modest moments, she even fancied the Deschanels as the Medicis of New Orleans.

"Who is your favorite Renaissance artist?"

"I can't pick one, because they each contributed in such powerful ways," Philip answered. "Most would say Botticelli, and certainly Venus and the Primavera are incomparable. But I can tell you the artist and the painting that made me both realize I was in the right and wrong place at the same time."

Colleen leaned forward, listening.

"Are you familiar with the story of Judith slaying Holofernes?"

"From the Book of Judith, which is part of the Apocrypha, and not the traditional Biblical texts."

Philip grinned. "I should remember never to be surprised with you. Holofernes was an Assyrian general whose antics threatened Judith, her loved ones, and her city. His desire for her was his weakness, which she exploited by entering his camp and decapitating him. This is too racy and violent for the men of the church, who can neither deny Judith's texts without denying those that have been deemed canon, nor include them without exposing that women are as formidable as men, if not more."

Colleen smiled from the corner of her mouth. "Yes, more."

"Many Renaissance artists took a stab at this scene, from Donatello to Caravaggio. I'd say you'd be hard-pressed to find a serious artist from this period who *didn't* tackle this. You can't enter a museum in Italy without coming across some rendering of Judith slicing the head off her would-be captor. The Uffizi alone has multiple renderings, and while I'm also partial to the especially violent and dark take by Gentileschi, the one I spent hours watching, alone, was the one by Peter Paul Rubens."

"He was Flemish, right?"

Philip nodded. "Flemish, yes. Very good. But he was heavily inspired by the Venetians, like Titian and Veronese. And he was an especial favorite of two kings, Philip IV of Spain and Charles I of England. You might say his style was both uniquely his, and uniquely belonging to all this major influences. Most of the renderings of Judith and Holofernes have a whimsical, inspirational feel. Good triumphing over evil. Have you seen Rubens' turn at this?"

Colleen hated to shake her head.

"Judith with the Head of Holofernes, it's called. I have a replica poster of this framed in my apartment that I'll show you one day, though I wish you could see it right now. It's not even considered among Rubens' most influential or well-known paintings, and when I tried to get my art professor to tell me more about it, he had very little to say, so I drew my own conclusions."

Colleen tried to stay focused on his words, but she didn't miss his casual promise to take her to his apartment, said as if there was nothing wrong with such a thing, as if she would agree, as if....

The waitress arrived with their wine, pouring them each a generous glass. Philip toasted Colleen without losing his focus.

"You see, Judith, here, is the dominant figure, which you think would be true in all renderings of her slaying her foe, but this is not true. She often takes a backseat to the crime. Here, she stands over him, all of her in rubenesque glory, a pure and enraged show of strength. Here, her servant is not a woman, but a *man*. That is what stood out to me when I first saw it, and on all my many subsequent visits, as I sat upon the bench and lost myself in Judith's victory. She's both beautiful and powerful, and the man servant is small and subservient. So many takes on Judith paint her as either violent or a seductress, but here she's just Judith, and she's incredible."

How Colleen wished she *were* standing in his apartment as he described this formative painting with more passion than she'd ever seen him attack science with. Or better yet, hands linked in the Uffizi in Florence, before the real thing. "You said this painting made you realize you were in both the right and wrong place at the same time."

Philip nodded. "That I did. Art scholars have a way of refusing to accept different interpretations of an artist's work. I've always believed that to be the ultimate beauty of *any* form of art, that even if you have a glimpse into the mind of the artist, you're still allowed to experience and interpret it in your own way. You'll find this mad, I'm sure, but I realized then that when it came to scholars, there was really no such thing as art at all. All scholars sought was a common thread and explanation to hang their hats on. To be right was more important than to be in the moment. You know what's worse? I have these inclinations, too. I need things to make sense, in a world where so much doesn't. Does that sound crazy?"

Colleen shook her head. She sipped at her wine, which was the best she'd tasted, and she felt so provincial in the shadow of this worldly man, who knew his wines and his art. "No, I understand what you're saying exactly, at least I think I do. I can look at the beauty of a flower garden and enjoy it, but sometimes that's ruined because I know exactly, because of science, why the roses have thorns, and how the colors came to be."

Philip's grin lit up his entire face. He slapped his leg. "Yes, yes! Exactly that, Colleen. Exactly that. I decided I was a better casual aficionado of art, because to tear it apart was to destroy the enjoyment. That's when I knew I had to follow my pragmatic side and return to the sciences."

"What we're good at isn't always the same as what we love."

"Wise words," Philip said. "But we can love what we are good at because we are good at it, no?"

Colleen thought about this. "Yes, there's joy in success. In feeling accomplished, and in knowing what you're capable of."

Philip nodded as he refilled both their glasses. "In reaching our potential, yes." The food arrived in that moment, and Colleen was glad of it, because she had nothing more meaningful to contribute and she worried he'd see that and see her as less than.

Using two spoons, he divided the generous plate of carbonara —he'd been right, this was no meal for one, and possibly not even two—to the two smaller plates provided. The smell was rich and delicious, and her stomach growled. This was not her mother's comfort cooking.

"Well?" he asked with a delighted look as he watched her tackle her food, using a spoon and fork to swirl the carbonara into a workable bite. She lifted the fork to her lips and sighed as the tastes erupted in her mouth. The oily saltiness of the pancetta was a delight against the softer flavors of the egg and cheese.

Colleen worked the food around in her mouth as quickly as she could without seeming indelicate. No one had ever watched her eat like this before. He'd folded his hands over the table, eyes regarding her with burgeoning interest. "Incredible," she offered after she swallowed.

"I knew you would love it," Philip said and began to eat as well. "Tastes just like the carbonara in Rome. I used to take the train there every weekend, because not even Florence does carbonara like the Romans."

"How did you find this place?"

"Same way I find anything. My evenings are quiet and sometimes lonely, and I drive around until I see something different. I seek out the places that are quieter, less established. Maybe I see these as art as well. Passion projects, opened from the love of cooking but without the desire for all the noise, all the marketing. This is the best Italian restaurant in New Orleans and no one knows about it."

"Doesn't that mean they'll eventually close?"

Philip shrugged. "I do my part by bringing my favorite people here."

"How many people have you taken here?"

Philip smiled. "Just you so far."

"I'm one of your favorite people?"

"One of a small few. I can get along with anyone, but it isn't often I find a kindred spirit."

"Now I'm a kindred spirit."

Philip reached across the table and took her hand in his. She'd been holding her fork, but it dropped to the plate with a clank. "When I said you weren't like the others who come in and out of my life at Tulane, I meant it. I'm a very private man, Colleen. I don't seek out company if I don't think the person can bring something new to my life. The day I heard you talk so passionately about the reason you chose to go to medical school... you were talking to your sister, I believe..."

Colleen felt the blood drain away from her face. "Evangeline. You were there?"

"Well, it *is* my office," he said. "Don't look like that."

"Like what?"

"Afraid of me. Of what I will think of you."

"I'm not," she lied. Her hand was damp with sweat now, but he hadn't released it.

"Not many scientists are brave enough to admit they believe there's more to this world. More to our minds, which are incredible and are *still* not fully understood. It isn't foolish or misguided to think they might be capable of more. Of forcing energy into heals, or reaching deep into the mind of another to see what's there."

Her heart raced so hard her limbs tingled. "Do you believe that?"

"I believe just because we haven't discovered something doesn't mean it isn't possible. I believe in the possibility of the unknown. And as it is, I have something of an interest in the extra senses humans possess, just as you do."

Not possibly, not remotely for the same reasons. "Have you ever... met someone who pushed this belief along?"

"You."

Colleen recoiled, and he dropped her hand as she fell back into her seat. What could he mean by this? What did he want?

"Simply, you remind me to never stop learning. To step outside what I know to be true and seek to find bigger truths." Philip reached his hand across the tiny table and cupped Colleen's cheek. Her eyes closed at the rush of emotional chills coursing through her, and when she opened them, he'd leaned across the table. His lips met hers, soft and inviting, and then he deepened the kiss, wrapping his other hand through her hair.

"You're not my student anymore," Philip said, breathless, as he settled back into his own seat. "I'd never pressure you toward something you didn't want. But I'm going to leave you with an address and a date two weekends from now. And if you're there, I promise you'll walk away knowing more about yourself than you could ever learn wholly on your own."

EVANGELINE CHEWED AT HER NAILS. She paused when Colleen stopped talking. "Wait, that's it?"

"Is that not enough?" Colleen wore a look of pure torment.

"What's the problem?"

"The problem is he is my senior, and I am his subordinate!"

"I'm gonna have to side with the prof on this one, sister. Technically, he's not your teacher anymore, and you're volunteering to help him now, not for credit. Tell me this, have you ever had a conversation like this with Rory?"

"It's not fair to compare them."

"Why?"

"Because they're nothing alike!"

"Exactly," Evangeline said. "Exactly. Colleen, look, you've always been a weirdo. I mean that with love. Poor Rory never stood a chance, and most men your age won't fare any better. Philip is on your level, even if he is twice your age, but who cares about that? He'll have a nice pension when he dies and you'll still be young enough to remarry."

"Stop," Colleen said, but she was smiling now.

"You have my advice. Go for it. Don't let your inner old woman keep you from something that might make you happy. And since you're here, we need to talk about the gold digger coming after our brother."

"Cordelia?"

"Cordelia? No! I'm talking about Augustus and Ekatherina."

"Who is Ekatherina?"

"Seriously?"

"Yes, seriously! Am I supposed to know?"

Evangeline rolled her eyes. "Your turn to settle in for a story."

TEN
IT'S THAT TIME

Charles had two meetings that day, as summer wound to fall, and because he expected neither to go well, he was not disappointed.

Colin asked him to come by Sullivan & Associates when he was in New Orleans. *Call ahead,* he said, because he had one year of law school ahead of him still and wasn't yet a regular in the family firm. You wouldn't have known it, with how serious he took the firm and everything that happened there. *Dad wants to talk to you, about business, but I'd like to see you, too, so I'll tag along.*

Colin Sullivan Sr. rarely had occasion to summon Charles to the law firm for business. He could count on two fingers the times he'd gone down by himself, and not tagging along with his father or mother. The first had been when his father died. He was eleven and legally not old enough to sign anything, but Colin Sr. explained that the acceptance of the family estate and position of heir was a symbolic gesture that was meant to bestow a sense of duty on the signer. Charles had signed the non-legally binding document with all the seriousness the task demanded, thinking of how they'd watched the somber video of Jack Kennedy's widow standing nearby when Johnson took on the duties of the nation.

The second was when he'd turned eighteen and the deed to Ophélie had formally been signed over to him. Ophélie, and several dozen other properties scattered across the state, all of which meant so little to him when it would have meant the world to someone else.

He should have gone down a third time, after turning twenty-one, when his trust opened up for his use, but he'd talked them into wiring the money to his account and having the paperwork delivered by courier.

But he was past all major milestones in the management of the estate, so he had no idea why they wanted to see him now.

Charles hadn't seen Colin since the wedding. They were back now from their honeymoon to Paris, which Charles knew had been Catherine's idea through and through. Paris was a dream to her, like so many other futures she'd cast aside in favor of safety and security.

He climbed the dark green carpeted steps, ascending into the law office that had maintained all markers of its old world charm. Desks of oak and mahogany, men traversing the space in crisp seersucker suits. Colin explained once that this was all intentional, to provide a timeless comfort to their clients, to which Charles had replied, *of course it's fucking intentional; nothing looks like this accidentally*.

Colin Sr. and Colin Jr. awaited him in the boardroom, which he could have found on his own, but a lovely young secretary had been perched in reception to bring him back.

"Thank you, darling," he said with a wink, enjoying her small grin and flushed cheeks.

Charles shut the door behind him.

"Mr. Sullivan." He shook Colin Sr.'s hand, then turned to his friend. "You're looking nice and tan, Colin."

"We extended the trip by a few days and spent time at a beach in the south of France. I must admit, it would have never occurred to me, but Catherine is full of ideas, and she keeps me on my toes."

She kept me on my knees. "So, what's this about?"

Colin Sr. gestured for Charles to sit. He loosened the top button of his sport coat and sat down himself. "I believe you know where your money comes from?"

Charles snickered. "Is this a quiz? I was never good at memorization."

"No, but, you see, that's why we're here. To gauge what your level of interest and desired involvement is, in the business side of the estate. Or, more to the point, how we continue to not only protect your money but grow it. Your father took a great interest in how the sausage is made, so to speak. He attended meetings, was involved in key decisions, and even redirected us from time to time."

"Business side of the estate?" Charles felt suddenly like a great fool. He'd never considered where the money came from, only that it was there. Had always been there, long before him, and would be there long after him. That they were the wealth of old money seemed to be the only pertinent fact involved. It had never once occurred to him there might be work involved in sustaining this.

And now that he considered it, it was obvious what an idiotic assumption this had been.

Where Colin Sr. seemed confused at Charles' confusion, Colin's eyes indicated he understood it implicitly. "The Deschanel money, as you know..." And Charles knew in that moment that Colin had inserted those three words, *as you know*, to save him from his growing horror of ignorance. What did he *think* August had been doing in his office, all those hours, all that time? "Comes from four sources primarily. Over two billion dollars in real-estate investments, which are comprised of both the steady revenue of equity and a re-investment of dollars into properties that are then sold for double the investment or more. Second are a complicated series of investment opportunities, large and small. The level of detail involved in maintaining these would likely not interest you, but there's another three billion in this careful dance of trading and monitoring. Third, the Deschanels own another half billion worth of interest in various banks, hospitals, and even smaller firms. Lastly, we've had success lately in fronting venture capital dollars, of which we have quadrupled investments made. Your family's net worth is just over seven billion dollars, Charles. Other than the reinvestment of some capital to keep the growth where it is, at over twenty percent per annum these past few years, most of that could be liquidated if the need arose, not that we expect it to. All the properties that are bestowed into the family upon maturity are owned outright by the estate and transferred to the bequeathed outright as well, so are not counted in the net worth estimate. As well, all trust fund dollars are kept separate, so anything paid out to your siblings, say, is protected. I could give you estimates on that as well."

Charles' head spun. He was glad to be seated. No one had ever bothered to explain any of this to him, and even now, he didn't know what half of it meant. He couldn't blame his father, who didn't expect to die before he could pass the baton. Nor could he exactly be mad at Irish Colleen, for what the hell did she know about any of this?

"Now that you're less than a year from your wedding, and hopefully soon after, the birth of your heir, we felt it prudent to see if you wanted to be part of everything, or continue to let us run it in your stead. It's that time." Colin Sr. watched him with a kind but hawkish smile.

"Can I think about it?"

Both men laughed. "Think about it? Charles, the estate is yours, to enjoy without disruption," said Colin Sr.

"If you decide nothing should change, then nothing will," Colin added. "With help from the accounting team we hired just *for* this, we've more than doubled your family's money over the years. We're good at this, even if it seems unusual to have your lawyers handle all your financial interests as well. So what we're saying is, this is all yours, and if you want to know more, or to get involved, we're here to help with that. But if you'd rather not burden yourself, and instead focus on growing your new family, or anything else, really, that's okay, too."

Charles knew what both of them were thinking; Colin Sr., with his aged wisdom; Colin Jr., with the smug satisfaction of having landed the only woman Charles had ever loved, even if he was blissfully unaware. They had called him here not because they thought he'd say yes, but because they knew they must. A check the box and a close of the folder.

Knowing this didn't change his current situation, though. He had no time to think about any of this. He was meeting Cordelia in thirty minutes, and if he bungled his plan, his whole life was forfeit. There was no way he could back out of this himself. He'd appeared before his mother at his lowest and given her his word, and it would be easy to break it to anyone else, but not her. For the first time in his life, she was proud of him.

But if Cordelia refused to marry *him*...

Charles stood. He channeled his father. "Thank you, gentlemen. You're right, I have a lot ahead of me in the coming months, but that doesn't mean this isn't important as well. I'll give it serious thought and be in touch."

CORDELIA SAT ALONE at a table situated dead center of the downstairs dining area of Galatoire's. If she'd applied mathematics to the decision she couldn't have positioned herself more centrally, and Charles struggled to understand the message she was sending.

"Hi," he said as he took his seat. His hands fumbled with what they were supposed to be doing. Should he shake her hand? Embrace her? He could kiss her, would kiss her, if she were anyone else. He shuddered at both the thought of making contact with the frigid bitch now, or ever.

If he didn't sort this out, he'd be touching her indefinitely. Or, at least until one of them finally leaped off the Crescent City Connection.

Cordelia turned her cheeks to the right and left, catching the invisible kisses that never came, then settled back into her chair, spine as rigid as he'd found her moments earlier.

"I'm here," she said. Her pinched mouth hardly moved with her words. Large, brown doe eyes blinked without emotion, eyes that would be pretty on anyone else. "Now, you'll tell me why."

"We're going to be married. Shouldn't we get to know each other?"

Cordelia's dead eyes blinked for several agonizing seconds. "You have a different perception of what this marriage means than I do, it seems."

Charles had the urge to strip to the nude in front of everyone, just to see if he could get anything more from her than the frozen, disabused look that seemed permanently plastered to her gaunt face.

"No, I don't think I do," Charles said. He ran his hand over the stubble on his chin, which he'd left for her benefit, just one more signal she was marrying a mess and there was still time to correct course. "I'd be more surprised if we had even one thing in common."

Cordelia's mouth smiled, but her eyes maintained their lifeless gaze. "We do have one thing in common. We'd both rather be dead than married to one another."

Charles had to remind himself not to feel wounded by such a strong comment. Even from her, it was a sting to the ego. She should be so damn lucky. He was worth seven fucking billion dollars. "I don't intend to be dead, so let's make the best of it, huh?"

Cordelia transferred her gaze off to the corner of the room, not looking at anything in particular so much as avoiding giving Charles more attention. He'd known women like her. Maybe not *exactly* like her, but he knew the tactic.

"Since you're going to be a Deschanel, there's some things you should know about us." He pushed forward, before he could lose his nerve. The nagging lilt of Irish Colleen appeared in his ear, like the angel upon his shoulder, reminding him that these secrets were not his to share. Not yet. Those were the rules, even if rules had never been his thing.

Fuck rules, if rules put him in the bedroom with this horrid creature.

"We're a little different," he said. "Not different in the way you might describe your drunk uncle."

"I get it." Her expression was worse than the eye-roll he heard behind her words. "You're *special*."

"You don't get it." He flexed his hands under the table, wondering where the hell the waitress was so he could order a cognac. "Here, let me show you."

Cordelia raised a brow, but she couldn't look less interested.

"I want you, in your head, to think of a number between one and ten thousand. Any number, but you need to really fixate on this number and nothing else, when I say go. Okay?'

"Whatever."

"I'm serious. Focus on a number."

"Sure. Fine."

"Go."

Charles so seldom performed this trick that he worried for a moment he might fail. Unlike the rest of his siblings, with their depth of abilities that were useful in all sorts of circumstances, his parlor trick was hardly much of anything. For the heir, he'd sure gotten the shaft.

"Ready for me to guess?"

Cordelia shrugged.

"Eight hundred and nine."

The smug look faded away. She didn't confirm his victory, but she didn't need to.

"Don't look so constipated, Cordelia. I don't make other people's thoughts my business unless they have something interesting in there." He cheered internally at the small shift of the upper hand. He had her attention now. "But that's nothing compared to what my family can do."

"It was a lucky guess," she said weakly.

"There's no such thing as a lucky guess when you're a Deschanel. No such thing as making a guess at all. All seven billion dollars to my name was a result of knowing *exactly* where to fucking put the money." *Even if I haven't a fucking clue about any of it.*

Cordelia grunted and folded her arms. He didn't read her mind this time, but sensed acutely her regret in coming to see him, which grew like compound interest. He didn't have much time.

"Augustus, my brother, he's an illusionist. He can make you see or think whatever he wants. You might think you like chocolate, but, lady, you'll be singing the praises of vanilla if it suits him."

She rolled her tongue around in her mouth.

"Colleen and Evangeline? Healers, both of them. Small, big, doesn't matter. They've saved the lives of all of us a few times over. They just put their hands on you and you're like brand-new, just like that."

"Right."

"Maureen? Communes with the dead. She's never alone, because she has my dad, my other sister, Maddy, who's gone now, and, oh yeah, this teacher she used to fuck."

"Charming."

"Then there's my baby sister, Lizzy, who can see the future. I guarantee you she'll see yours as soon as you meet her. She's homeschooled now, because she kept predicting the deaths of all her classmates' family members. You can see how that might put a crimp in her popularity."

Cordelia's wax expression shifted slightly. "Just deaths? Is that all she predicts?"

Charles tried not to smile. He had her now. "No, those are just the ones that piss everyone off the most. But Lizzy can see *all* kinds of things, good and bad. Anything, really. Anything at all."

"You're right, you are special." Cordelia ignored the waiter as he came to, finally, take their drink order. She stood up. "How fortunate for me."

"Where are you going?"

"What a fascinating lie to tell. And why, I have to ask myself, for no one lies for the sport of it."

"I'm not lying! I don't even have the imagination for a lie like that!"

"My prediction? Your desire for happiness is beginning to eclipse your call to duty, and you're hoping to weasel out of it, by way of me, but you would only make such a miscalculation because you don't know me at all, which, ironically, was the guise by which you got me to show up to begin with. I don't know whether I should congratulate you or vomit on your Italian leather shoes."

"I don't understand a word you just said."

This smile was the first he believed. "Of course you don't."

"What I'm telling you is completely fucking true. I would have told you after we were married, because that's when spouses are read-in to this shit, but I happen to think telling people *after* they're already committed is too-little-too-fucking-late, and more than a little unfair. I wanted you to have a chance to know what you're getting into."

"I know what you wanted, Charles. If you're going to be a deserter to your own cause, you'll have to take those cowardly steps on your own."

Cordelia's kitten heels clicked hard against the checkered floor as she left him sitting alone, the eyes of everyone around their table drawn to what they could only perceive to be him being stood up. Him. Charles Deschanel. Heir to New Orleans.

Which was exactly what she wanted them all to think.

The heinous bitch.

MAUREEN TRIPPED over her bed at the shock of the unannounced visitor.

"Jesus, Charles!" she cried. She righted herself and crawled back up over the comforter. She looked to her right and hissed, "You hush."

"Who are you talking to?"

"This dickhead Jean, who raped his sister. He's our ancestor, and he hates it when I take the Lord's name in vain."

"Sounds like an aces guy." Charles knitted his brows. "Are you busy?"

"Didn't seem like you cared about that when you barged right in without even a knock. What if I was having sex?"

"Under this roof? Doubtful."

Maureen glared. "You did."

"I'm an adult, and this is my house."

"In age maybe," Maureen muttered. She hitched her miniskirt, which had crawled up in her fall from the bed, down over her thighs. It wasn't the most practical outfit for just hanging around, but she was expecting Connor's brother, Thomas, today, and she had to keep him guessing just enough.

"Who else is in the room?"

"What? You and me."

Charles planted his hands on his hips. "You know what I mean, don't be dippy."

"Oh." She sometimes forgot she'd shared this secret with him, and sometimes regretted that fact. But she wasn't worried about him telling anyone, either, and she wished he were easier to talk to, so she could unburden herself. "Right now? Um, well, Jean is over there giving me the glare of the blasphemer, as I think of it, and Maddy was here a minute ago, and I think..." She looked around. "No, she went somewhere else. I don't know where they go when they're not here, don't ask me." Mercifully, the baby was quiet today. It wasn't much, but she'd take a day of silence. "Daddy, too."

"Dad? He's here?" Charles looked around as though he could see August if he strained just right.

Maureen nodded.

"Good." Charles pulled out the chair from her desk and straddled it backward. "I need you to ask him something for me."

"You... what?"

"I need your help, Maureen. I need Dad's advice, and there's no other way for me to get it."

"I don't know..."

"If I can help my son, I want to," August said. He stood so near to Charles, hand hovering over his shoulder, that Maureen was panicked at the thought that Charles might look up and actually *see* him.

"Please. It's my life we're talking about, not something stupid."

Maureen still smarted from the reaming her mother had given her over her helping Elizabeth. Things had been going well before that, not great, but well, and now she was again persona non grata among the Deschanels. The black sheep. The failure.

She'd tried to find less risky ways of proving she could be useful. Two days ago, she'd driven into New Orleans to see Augustus, which was a bad decision—she was grounded from driving indefinitely, and waited for her mother to be out for the day with errands—that had potential to lead to good results. She stood in front of him in his big office, her big brother looking so important now, and not at all the soft, sweet boy she'd played with in their garden, and pleaded with him to give her a job. He'd sighed, looked around, and said summer was a slow time, and that she could come back and see him in fall and he'd find something. But fall might as well be a decade, for as miserable as she was, once again relegated to the role of *Failure Maureen*.

"I'm going to marry this miserable bitch, and I just need to know *why*. I need to know why this is my fucking future, Maureen. Dad knows why."

"Maureen, please, let me talk to my son."

"Daddy, this is between Huck and me."

"He's here? You're really talking to him?" Charles looked at once like he might pass out or cry.

This might be it, her bid for usefulness, and there was nothing bad that could come of it. No missing sister. No forced abortion. Just Charles, looking to her, as the only one who could give him what he wanted.

He'd never asked her for anything before.

"Okay," she said. "He can hear you, so just... I don't know, say what you want, or ask what you want, and I'll tell you what he says."

"Good. Good." Charles kicked the chair away and leaned against the desk. He gnawed on his knuckle, then rapped it against the wood. "Hi, Dad. I miss you. A whole lot."

Maureen listened, and then said, "Dad said he misses you more than anything."

Charles bit down on his knuckle again. "I don't know if I can do this."

"It's okay," Maureen said, but sounded about as soothing as wiping a foot across gravel. "What do you want to ask him?"

"I want to know what to do about this situation with Cordelia. I know Dad knows what I'm talking about."

"I do know," August said, and Maureen relayed everything he said as he went on. "I do know, Charles, and it's the result of one of my deepest regrets in life. I never should have made a deal with that devil Franz! I should have walked away, when I could... I wasn't even involved, but I stood by him, and every second I stayed made me more complicit. And then I was in a corner, with no choice but to make a promise. I'd do anything to turn back the clock and fix this, because you'll only meet misery if you marry into that family. But if you do not, then the rest of this family will know a much greater misery."

Charles' face paled. He dropped his hand, and his mouth parted. "So there is a story. I knew it. I fucking *knew* it! I need to know. I deserve to know, if this is my burden now."

"He won't say," Maureen said. She gave her father a hard look. "Huck is right, Daddy. Hell's bells, if you put him in this situation, then you need to tell him why he has to live with it!"

"I can't," August said, hanging his head low. "My son's memory of me is all the connection we have left. I won't tarnish that."

"That's a bunch of bullshit," Maureen said.

"What? What is he saying?"

"Nothing useful," she said, eyes still burning holes in her father. "Nothing useful at all."

"Dad!" Charles cried. "Why won't you tell me? You did this to me, so why won't you tell me?"

"Ask your mother, so I don't have to see your eyes when you learn the truth," August said and dissolved from the room.

Maureen repeated this, and then said, "I'm sorry. He's gone."

"Fuck!"

"Yeah, it's total bullshit, Huck. I'm so sorry. Maybe there's another way to get you out of this marriage."

"Any fucking ideas?" His words died in the air between them, too deflated to cut through the sadness.

"No, but don't forget, I'm the survivor of the family. If anyone can help you figure this out, it's me."

"Yeah? I'd owe you for life."

Maureen smiled. "I just want what you want. To not be shackled by this damn family and their terrible choices for the rest of my life."

FALL 1973

VACHERIE, LOUISIANA
NEW ORLEANS, LOUISIANA

ELEVEN
TANTRA

Philip was an excellent cook, and he loved to surprise Colleen with something new after each of their marathon lovemaking sessions. Today, he woke her with a quail quiche, which he confessed to have prepared ahead of her arrival so all he had to do was pop it in the oven.

Colleen was a little embarrassed at how she always fell asleep after their bedroom play. She was half Philip's age and should have twice his stamina, but his experience shone through every touch of his hand and flit of his tongue. Colleen had only ever been with one man, and Rory's experiences and hers had been equally matched. They were kids, fumbling through the motions, guessing where their passion might lead instead of taking confident charge and guiding it through to completion. Philip knew precisely what he was doing. No move was accidental. No gesture wasted.

A week after their relationship had taken a sexual turn, a line they could never re-cross, Philip introduced her to something he called tantric sex. She was woefully unfamiliar with even the term, which was not a position she was used to or liked, but he was happy to demonstrate. He coached her through the breathing exercises meant to prolong satisfaction, and the sex that was not sex at all, not until the end when, after hours of this, she exploded with an orgasm she thought might kill her.

Colleen needed to research this practice, to understand it better so that she was not always the consummate student with Philip, but was afraid to approach a librarian with such a book request.

Later, he told her he was a secret Buddhist; that he attended mass every Sunday like a good Catholic, but struggled mightily with the shame Catholics were meant to feel over every little thing. *With Buddhism, it's quite simple. You get from the world what you send out into it, good or bad. Your goal is not to please a vengeful god, but to attain individual enlightenment, by seeking those things that go beyond the material.*

Colleen didn't say that Buddhism had become something of a trend these days, with followers springing up right and left, crawling from the woodwork as if they'd been there all along. He was not as unique as his words and eyes seemed to convey. And yet, his passion for it rang genuine.

A week after that, Philip brought something even more foreign to her into the relationship. She was afraid when he brought out the small mahogany box, filled with baggies of white powder. This was not her realm. She was fine being the stick-in-the-mud who did everything the boring way.

I'm not a druggie, Colleen. I save this only for lovemaking, to heighten the experience for both of us. Do you trust me?

If he'd been anyone else, Colleen would have snatched her clothes from the settee and run far away. Her will was ironclad, and she had never felt the pull to peer pressure as many of her peers had. She knew who she was.

But so did Philip, and his self-assured confidence in the way he both gently encouraged yet also remained hesitant until he knew she was okay to proceed. She'd never seen or heard of him doing drugs and had no reason to believe he was lying to her now. He hadn't led her astray yet... he'd awakened her to so many new experiences, new heights of being.

Colleen had lain back, guided by his hands, which first pressed her softly into the pillow and then, running down her bare flesh, parted her legs. She had the urge to snap her legs closed, afraid of the exposure; the vulnerability. But his eyes implored her to trust him, and so she had.

Philip had dipped one finger in the baggie of coke and then nestled it between her legs, right atop those bundles of nerves she'd never known contained so much potential. It was one thing to study the physiology of an orgasm. Another entirely to be amidst the experiment.

He dabbled some powder on his thumb and lifted to his nose, inhaling and sniffling as he rubbed his thumb back and forth. He then offered the same to Colleen, and later what she remembered most was how little she'd hesitated in this moment. The burst of adrenaline filled her from head to toe, and for a single moment she understood Charles, finally.

Philip handed her a slice of quiche and nestled into the side of the bed. She pulled the sheet over her bare chest. It was one thing to be exposed in the heat of the moment, but with the passion died down to coals, she felt as she had when she'd awaken hungover after her first episode with alcohol.

"What are you thinking?" he asked.

"Nothing, I just woke up."

"Compliments to the chef?" he teased, and it took her a minute, but then she too laughed.

"Actually, I was thinking that this apartment needs a woman's touch."

"You've been coming here for weeks and you just now make this observation?"

Colleen took a bite of the quiche, which was wonderful, as he was, as everything he touched was. "No, I think I always noticed, but now it stands out at me." There was almost nothing in the apartment that made it feel lived-in. No art—though he'd said he had quite the collection, and she had really looked forward to the Judith painting—none of the touches that separate the sterility of a hotel room from the warmth of a home.

Philip set his plate aside. "I see. Well, the truth is, I don't spend much time here, unless I'm with you."

"Don't you live here?"

"I sleep here, but I still live in my house on Napoleon."

Colleen dropped her fork to the plate. "Isn't that where your wife lives?"

Philip bristled, but it was so quick she almost missed it. Almost. "No, not exactly. The house is only blocks from the boys' school, and we trade off who stays there with them during the week. They'll be in high school next fall, and then we'll sell the house and figure out the best way to co-parent."

He'd never talked about his children with her, though she knew he had teenage twin boys. But she didn't know anything else about them. Not even their names.

"But you're never there together?"

"Sometimes we're there together."

Colleen didn't know what her next question should be. She knew what she wanted it to be. But she couldn't ask that, not when it seemed obvious to her that this entanglement of theirs wasn't meant to come with bindings or rules.

Philip sat up taller. "You want to know if she knows about you. If she cares."

Colleen didn't say a word.

"Colleen, I haven't slept with my wife in years. That we're still on speaking terms is nothing short of a miracle. We figured out a system so we could care for our sons, but that's it. She doesn't know about you, and I'm not telling her, because I don't want her to harass you."

"Harass me? Do you really think she would?"

He shrugged. "It wouldn't be the first time." He lay down next to her and pulled her into him. "Look, I know why you have questions, but there's nothing to get yourself worked up about here. That's what I love about you... you understand the world in a way most can't comprehend. If I tell you my broken marriage is complicated, you understand exactly what I mean."

Colleen didn't understand exactly what he meant, and this felt like another failure, so she only nodded.

"I don't have a life outside of the school." He kissed her, lingering. "Outside of you. My life consists of lectures, soccer practice, and then unwinding in your beautiful arms. There isn't time for anything else. And you know about that, too, don't you? You've set aside your passions to be the pillar holding up your family. We're so much alike, you and I."

How she wished that to be true. In Philip's eyes, she finally saw the reflection of herself that she'd always imagined.

And now in the fall, she saw him only in this small, Spartan apartment. Her summer help didn't catch too much attention, as the enrollment was so much smaller in comparison to the other terms, but in fall, the aide role was coveted. She could no longer hold onto it without putting him under the microscope, not when she had no further classes of his.

It didn't help that she'd come upon him standing over the shoulder of his new aide, a pretty blonde. She couldn't hear what they were saying, but their smiles were equally bright, and even with her limited experience in flirting, she understood body language and felt like an intruder. Nor did it help that he snapped back in alarm when he saw Colleen enter the room.

Stop. Just stop. You're a chronic over thinker. You steal your own joy!

Philip kissed her again. "I have to get to class." Another kiss. "Mmm, but what I wouldn't do to stay in bed with you all day."

"I have class, too," she said, but that was a lie, and she feared he's see right through it. He might be open-minded about the metaphysical, but she couldn't tell him about her family. She couldn't tell him she had a tea date with her Aunt Ophelia and Evangeline, because she no longer trusted herself or her own ability to discern right from wrong.

"Tonight, then?" He was already dressing.

"I can't tonight."

"Is it your other boyfriend?"

Colleen looked shocked, and only when he laughed did she realize that, again, she'd missed the joke.

Tonight was the quarterly Collective Council meeting, yet another thing she couldn't tell him, and with a sting of self-righteousness, realized she didn't want to. If he could have his secrets, so could she.

Philip, dressed now, crawled over the sheets on all fours toward her. He fell back on his feet and reached for her face with both hands. "You are the most incredible woman I've ever known, Colleen."

The creeping venom, that horrible green jealousy she loathed in others, slinked back where it had come from. She kissed him with her whole heart, and was once again his.

COLLEEN FOUND Ophelia after several loops around the luscious gardens of The Gardens. She did a double take at the woman in scarlet hunched over among the vast sea of red lantanas.

"*Tante*!" Colleen said with a laugh. "You shouldn't be out here laboring like this. You have gardeners to handle these tasks."

Ophelia pulled off her red sun hat and regarded her niece

with something bordering annoyance. "Are you suggesting I lie down and die, child?"

"Colleen doesn't know any better than to stick her nose where it doesn't belong," sang Evangeline as she skipped up behind them, her boots announcing her long before her words.

"My dearest Evangeline, your hair continues to grow even as you do not."

"Thank you, *Tante*," Evangeline replied. She bounced her curls in one hand.

"But we're here to talk about your sister's most recent exploits, are we not?" Ophelia cast aside her hat like a Frisbee and mopped her brow with the back of her gardening glove.

"Exploits." Colleen's lip curled. "That makes me sound like I'm up to no good."

"Well? Aren't you?"

THEY SETTLED in on the screened porch. The September heat made the outdoors untenable, but Ophelia had four fans going, and this felt much better than standing in the garden.

Aria, the young maid Ophelia had hired a few years back, brought out a pitcher of iced tea and some biscuits. Ophelia indulged herself first and let the young women serve themselves.

"You look good, *Tante*," Colleen said.

"I was going to say you looked better than before the pneumonia, but wasn't sure if that was taking it a step too far," Evangeline added.

Ophelia squinted at the younger girl before erupting into gravelly laughter. "Evangeline, dear, never lose your candor. Never, please. Where Colleen will tell me what she thinks I most wish to hear, you've always told me the truth."

"I don't lie to you," Colleen defended.

"Not lying is not a match for pure honesty."

"As it is, I *do* feel better. One of my doctors, bless the poor man, for I fired him for this comment, but he remarked to me that often the elderly will experience a burst of energy before the end. Well, I feel most assured that this is not the end. Not today, anyway."

Colleen wished that day would never come, but that was the foolish pining of a child.

"That doesn't mean I don't make the most of every precious second, though," Ophelia said. She drew her glass, covered in dewy condensation, to her lips, both girls fixated on her shaky hand. When she caught them, she tsked them both. "So, let us get right to it. Our Colleen is enjoying time with her teacher in the Lord's way. He's twice her age and still married. Is that enough to catch me up?"

To hear it through such stark words made Colleen's joy assemble in the pit of her stomach.

"Yes, *Tante*," Evangeline said, when Colleen didn't. "And it wouldn't be typical Colleen if she wasn't worrying herself sick over it."

"No," Ophelia agreed. "The heart of the matter, then. Your worries, are they more centered around whether what you are doing is right or wrong? Whether he loves you? Whether he is lying about his relationship with the woman still legally his wife, and always mother of his children?"

"I suppose it's all of that," Colleen said. "And also none of that. I'm so conflicted, but I know this conflict is not so black and white for me. I've passed up many opportunities to follow my heart, or my more baser instincts, over what I knew to be right. But what has me so confused is that when I'm with him, it *feels* right, in a way things never did with Rory. I know you both think I'm foolish for caring so much about things like this, but the fact that he is my intellectual equal is an incredible draw for me. I feel, for once, like I'm with someone who is most like me."

Evangeline reached across the chairs and squeezed her hand.

"I don't think you're foolish for wanting a partner who brings out the best of what is already great in you," Ophelia said. "But it is foolish to believe there is only one man in the world capable of filling that void for you. Philip is only the first, Colleen. He doesn't need to be the last, or even the best."

"But what if he is?"

Ophelia's wrinkles formed a tight smile. "You are a sly one, and I can never tell when you are seeking conversation or divination."

Colleen looked away. She did this with her aunt, had always done this, where she rode the line, never daring to ask for her future, but not opposed to the idea of it accidentally slipping out from a misunderstanding of intention. "Today, I just want your advice."

"I find that hard to give when I've already seen your future."

"Oooh, let me guess, she marries Ryan O'Neal, after he reveals he's really, in real life, the same dreamy Harvard Law student he played in *Love Story*."

Ophelia and Colleen both looked at her as if she were an alien.

"He also has a professional curiosity about telepathy and other metaphysical disciplines," Colleen said. "He's not some hippie from the Haight, high on LSD. He's a thrice-degreed science professor whose work has been peer-reviewed many times over."

"People are curious about ghosts until they're haunted by one," Ophelia said.

"I'm only pointing out how hard it is for those who marry into this family to come to terms with what we are."

"Now you want to marry him?"

"No, that isn't what I meant!"

"You should think about what you do mean. I'll give you the

advice I'd give anyone in your situation, Colleen. You are no longer his student, and the ethics of that should not play into your decision here. The college might feel differently, but he is the one who needs to worry about that, not you. However... unhappy men cheat, but most never leave their wives."

"It isn't cheating if they're separated," Colleen said, ignoring the sound Evangeline made to her right. "They're still married because it makes it easier to care for their sons. They take turns living in the house so the boys don't feel abandoned."

Ophelia tilted her head to the side. She looked directly into Colleen's eyes. "Now that you've said it all aloud, does it feel more or less like bullshit?"

"You don't know him," Colleen said, and even that felt weak, and she thought herself weak, too, for saying it.

"Leena," Evangeline started, in her *I'm about to educate you, but it's really just love* voice. "Maybe you're right. Maybe he's got this arrangement with his wife for good reasons. But you wouldn't have pulled out the big guns"—she winked at Ophelia—"if you didn't have reason to doubt him. Now that you've gotten your sage wisdom of the ancients, which you're hesitant to take, I see only one path forward for you."

"Oh?"

"You have to do a little reconnaissance work. Figure out what is true that he's told you and what might not be."

"What are you talking about? Spying?"

Evangeline shrugged. "Desperate times, and all that."

Ophelia's sigh filled the room. "You're leaving for Scotland in less than a year, Colleen. Whatever you might be feeling, use this as your guide to temper yourself. Is this a man who will be waiting for you in four years?"

Colleen recoiled at what seemed less about him and more about her. Her ego stung. And why wouldn't he wait for her? Was she not worth waiting for?

"Don't get your hackles up with me, young lady. If you came to hear me sing his praises as your Prince Charming, you've come to the wrong place, and you knew that before you walked in." Ophelia reached for her cane and wobbled to a stand. "You want my advice? Here it is, Colleen. You already know the answer. Your gut has always known, and your gut doesn't steer you wrong. I challenge you to find one example of where leading with your gut led you false."

Evangeline nodded as though taking credit for the words.

"I have feelings for him. I think they're real," Colleen said helplessly.

"Bully for you," said Ophelia and hobbled back into the house.

TWELVE
STRANGE BEDFELLOWS

Charles resisted the engagement party with every last bit of authority he still possessed with his mother. She had her mind set on the tradition, despite how little regard she held the Deschanel traditions in. She was an anachronism of disgust and acquiescence, and it was as if August was guiding and encouraging her from the grave. Even Ophelia said, when she came over for a rare afternoon tea, *For the love of Pete, are you really going to put the poor boy through this, Colleen?*

Charles had no desire to make a bad situation worse, and, as Cordelia had said, their mutual hatred was the one thing they did have in common. He knew she was even less enthused about the party, so he'd called her ahead of time to see if she could work on her father.

"Misery acquaints a man with strange bedfellows," she'd replied.

"Huh?"

"Shakespeare. You must have heard of him. Then again..."

You might say I've heard of him. "Yeah, sure."

"I'll work on it," she said with her signature world-weary sigh

—one he was already so familiar with—and hung up the phone without another word, or goodbye.

Charles had no doubt of her commitment to seeing the party cancelled, but even her determined toxicity wasn't enough to stop this train from leaving the station.

For a woman who harbored such disdain for her husband's family and privilege, Irish Colleen had more contacts than a councilman's rolodex. All the wealthy Garden District, Mandeville, Metairie, and Uptown families were well represented, including the many branches of the Deschanels' own tree. The Sullivans were there, too, although they were a different brand of bourgeoisie, having earned their money the old-fashioned way. Many doors still remained closed to them, though on the arms of a Deschanel, they were welcomed anywhere. The Sullivans were possessed of a stubborn pride about who they were and their path to get there, and Charles knew they turned their noses up at the idea that the Deschanels were their access to many things. But it was the Sullivans who had been there for their family at their darkest hours. Not the Weatherlys, or the Conrads, or the Villeneuves. Charles would take a Sullivan over any of them, any day of the week.

Elizabeth said she counted over three hundred people strolling the grounds of Ophélie with their mint juleps and trails of gossip. Elizabeth wasn't one to embellish, so that sounded right to Charles, and it certainly *felt* right, as he couldn't even dip around a corner without someone appearing from nowhere to congratulate him or espouse their idea of sage advice on the subject of married life.

Dan Weatherly was the first. With a somber look more appropriate for a funeral, he'd clapped a hand on Charles' shoulder and with a tight smile said, "My man. My man. This doesn't have to be a death sentence. I've got you. We'll get a regular rotation of beauties that will help you forget all about that cold hag."

Charles didn't need Dan Weatherly's crude pimping to get laid and was sensitive to the insinuation. In fact, it had been at one of Dan's parties that one of these so-called beauties had mounted Charles while he was completely out of his mind, only to later end up giving birth to a Deschanel bastard that Charles had used all his brainpower to forget about.

Fuck Dan for making him think about that shit again.

Irish Colleen had gone all out for the event. No barn ladder they owned was tall enough to hang the garlands from the upper portico, or stringing the light from live oak to live oak—Charles knew this only because he'd seen her try—so she'd hired professionals to both decorate and cater the event. Thousands of lights blanketed the property when dusk descended. The decorators had woven lilies and orange lantana through the garland wrapped around every column of the house. The last time he'd seen Ophélie so dressed was when Irish Colleen had the wild and terrible idea to host cotillion there and forced Colleen and Madeline to go through the torturous process of becoming debutantes.

He'd done his level best to avoid more than a passing glance at Cordelia for the past two hours. No one seemed to notice that they weren't meandering the party together, arm in arm, as a couple in love would, and he wondered if everyone secretly knew how fucking miserable he was about the whole thing. Most of the advice he received, as people slipped an arm around his waist or shoulder, half-or-all-the-way drunk due to Irish Colleen's open bar sensibilities, were along the same vein as advice you'd give a man with a cancer diagnosis.

Jamie Sullivan: *Give and take. It's all give and take. Sometimes you give more than you take, but them's the breaks.*

Jerome Sullivan, his brother: *No one ever really tells you about marriage until you're in it, but it's really not so bad. Don't let anyone scare you.*

Claudius Broussard, who had married the infamous Blanche: *Listen, Charles, marriage is wonderful, of course, but you have to establish your dominance before it's taken from you. Women do that, and I don't think they mean it, or maybe they do, but you gotta know your ground before it can be walked all over.*

Pansy Guidry: *You treat that woman like a queen, Charles, ya hear? Don't let me go around hearing you ain't her king.*

Eugenia Fontenot: *Marriage is a beautiful blessing. Truly, a blessing.*

Wallace Fontenot, her husband, whispering out of her earshot: *Pick your battles, son. Be prepared to lose most of them.*

Pierce Guidry: *Once you have children, everything changes. Everything.*

Blanche Broussard, whose first two husbands died under mysterious circumstances: *Best of luck to you, darling. And remember, marriage doesn't have to be forever, unless you want it to.*

Ophelia Deschanel, (laughing): *Bless you, Charles. There's a reason I've never married.*

At one point, he'd let himself imagine his bride was Catherine and nearly replied that they didn't need to worry, they'd keep each other on their toes, always guessing, always happy. The comedown from this was worse than a break from coke, though, and instead he resigned himself to the truth with the reminder from that sad sack Weatherly that this wasn't the end of his sex life. His future wife wouldn't even hold it over his head. She'd probably be off doing the same, if she wasn't dead inside.

Someone rang the old plantation bell. Or several someones, he thought, because the cursed ancient thing was larger than a car. The crowds began filtering toward the rear of the house, to where the intricate parterre garden now housed dozens of benches and over a hundred folding chairs.

Charles hung out at the back of the unfolding events. Franz and Irish Colleen stood upon a small dais at the other end of the garden, both holding microphones. Franz looked pleased as punch, with a smile suggesting he'd stolen not one but all the cookies from the jar. Irish Colleen, on the other hand, wore the pained and uncomfortable look of someone who belonged where she was but wasn't quite certain how she'd gotten there, or why.

Franz cleared his throat and made to speak into his microphone, when tiny Irish Colleen stepped forward first. *That's right, Mama. This is your show.* "I want to thank you all for coming here today, to celebrate the marriage of my eldest, dear son, Charles, to the daughter of our old friend, Franz. Cordelia, I welcome you to our family with the open arms of a mother and ask you to look after my baby. And Charles..." She searched for him and failed to find him, hiding her frown in her next words, which were a touch less confident. "Charles, your father and I raised you to be a fair and dutiful husband, providing for your family in the way we taught you. Next summer, we'll be here again to watch the two of you say your sacred vows, and that will be the proudest day of my life." She blotted her eyes.

Augustus appeared at his left, cradling a whiskey. Charles gave him an approving look. "I've never seen you drink."

"Under the circumstances," Augustus said, without elaboration.

"Have you seen..." Charles stopped himself.

"Catherine?" Augustus nodded to the left. He tugged at his tie, loosening it. "Over there, other side of the garden, trying her best not to appear as if she's looking at you."

Charles chuckled to himself. The small victories were all he had left.

"She had a bit of a run-in with your fiancée earlier."

"She... *what?*"

Augustus grinned into his drink as he took another sip. "She tried to congratulate Cordelia, and Cordelia asked her just what was there to be so excited about? Catherine's feathers got a bit rankled, and she came to your stirring defense."

"Shit." Charles chanced a look at Catherine and caught her eye. She looked miserable. "Did Colin see?"

"He was there, but I don't think he made the connection, if that's what you're asking."

"That is what I'm asking."

"You're safe for now."

"Thank you, Colleen." Franz stepped not just forward but around Charles' mother. "We are joined here today, to celebrate the impending union..."

Charles zoned him out. He felt someone come up behind him and turned to see his baby sister. "Lizzy. Thank you for joining me for my sentencing."

Elizabeth snickered. "The whole family is a bunch of buffoons. Have you met the brother?"

"Oh, Darwin," Augustus said. "He's a charmer."

"You know him?" Charles asked.

"I know of him. He's not well regarded in the business world. No one will loan him a penny without his father in the room."

"Where's Cordelia?" Elizabeth looked around.

"Drowned in the river, one can hope," Charles murmured.

"Huck!" she chided. "That's never funny. What would be *funny* is if she got lost in the maze of sugarcane and starved to death."

Both Augustus and Charles gaped at her.

"Sorry to say, that's not her future," Elizabeth said under her breath and shoved the straw from her Coke in her mouth.

Everyone around them applauded, and the three joined in without knowing exactly why. Franz had finished his droning speech and now was asking if anyone else had well wishes for the couple.

Colin handed Catherine his drink and went to approach the podium, but was blown aside by Rory stumbling past him and stealing the microphone.

"What a party!" he cried out, tripping over his own feet. Franz steadied him and then retreated quickly.

"Jesus Christ, we need to stop him." Colleen appeared. "He's had way too much to drink. He never drinks like this. I don't know what he's thinking."

"I'm sure he's just high on love," Charles quipped.

Colleen raised both of her judgmental brows on him. "He can't hold his liquor. He'll make a fool of himself, and possibly you."

Charles crossed his arms and swirled his drink. "That's exactly what this party needs!"

Colleen grunted and turned to Augustus. "Are you going to stop him?"

Augustus shrugged with a *and just what am I supposed to do about it?* look.

"Only a Deschanel could command an audience like this!" Rory went on. "All the important people are here. Would be a great time for someone to drop a bomb."

A ripple of silence passed through the crowd. Murmurs followed.

"Yeah, well, who knew Charles would be marrying Cordelia Hendrickson? Who even knew they were *dating*?" Rory finished off his drink and tried to set it aside, but there was nothing to place it on and it dropped to the ground. "Yeah. Yeah, marriage. Marriage, man. It's a beautiful thing. It's a mystery... and you know what else is a mystery to me? I'm talking a real bona fide mystery, the kind that Agatha What's-Her-Face might write about..."

"Christie," Colleen whispered with a disapproving sigh.

"What's a mystery to *me* is how my brother married Catherine, and now Charles is marrying Cordelia, but *just a few months ago* Charles and—"

Augustus pulled the microphone from Rory and passed it back to his mother before ushering the drunk man off the stage. Charles hadn't even noticed him leave his side, and the matter was dealt with so swiftly that Charles hardly had time to process that Rory had very nearly, almost revealed Charles and Catherine's secret. One more word... had Augustus arrived even a second later... and at the very least Charles and Catherine would have some explaining to do.

At worst, Catherine and Colin's lives would have come crashing down, and Charles' with it.

Augustus delivered Rory to Colin, who tugged at his brother and escorted him somewhere out of sight. Catherine's wide, terrified eyes darted between her Sullivan family and Charles, unsure of where to land.

"All right! Who else?" Franz asked.

Someone else, Charles never saw who, went up to give their speech for the couple. He didn't see or notice because Catherine shuffled over to him, trying to get to him quickly without drawing attention. Augustus was right behind her and, wordlessly, provided a barrier with his stance, and Colleen, quietly, joined him. Elizabeth slipped in beside them. Catherine disappeared behind their shield and wiped at her eyes.

"I shouldn't have come," she sobbed.

"Probably not," Charles agreed, but, briefly, squeezed her hand in his and dropped it. It fell back to her side. He regretted it immediately.

"How can you marry her, Huck? She's horrible. She's..."

"Not you? Could have been you, but you two-timed with Colin and then married him, for reasons that still make no goddamn sense," he said and didn't care if his siblings heard. By now they must know. "Am I supposed to wait for you to get tired of him? Is that it? Or if you can't have me, then no one can?"

"No... no, that's not what I meant..."

"Then what, Cat? What did you mean? I'd make it quick, before Colin figures out where you went."

"You deserve better, that's all. You deserve someone who will love you and not marry you because they have to."

"You just described Colin, you know that? That's what you did, and you don't think he deserves better?"

"Colin's back and looking for Cat," Maureen said, appearing from apparently nowhere to round out the protection.

"Go to your husband, Catherine," Charles said. "Stop worrying about me and start worrying about him."

Cat opened her eyes wide and blinked to push away the tears. She sniffled and leaned in. "You think you understand me, and my choices, and what I've done, but you have no idea. You sit there in judgment, when you once loved me, and think you know it all. You don't know a thing, Charles. Not a thing."

Catherine broke through the barrier between Augustus and Colleen and disappeared into the crowd.

"She's gotta learn some tact, Huck," Colleen said. "She can't be doing this at your engagement party. If not for your sake, then for her own."

"Stay out of it," Charles barked and left them all, heading for the river, for a spot none of them knew; a place where he was not in this terrible situation and his heart wasn't broken.

ELIZABETH COULD NOT HAVE SAID why she followed Cordelia into the horse barn. She didn't trust the wretched woman, and there was nothing *in* the barn these days, certainly not horses, or anything useful for that matter. *I just want to talk,* Cordelia said, but when had those words ever been safe?

She stepped into the wide, empty space, which smelled faintly of old hay and not much else. When she reached the center of the floor, she heard the whoosh of the old double doors closing behind her and then the thud of the latch striking. Most of the light disappeared, except the few swashes of moonlight streaming through gaps in the wood siding.

Elizabeth turned. That weirdo, Darwin, grinned at her as he leaned into what was both the only entrance and exit.

"What's going on?"

"We just want to talk," Darwin said, and his smile was now like that cat, in *Alice in Wonderland*, and she didn't trust anything about it. Not a thing.

"Yes, don't be alarmed, Elizabeth. There's nothing to be afraid of." She turned toward this second voice, another man, and found it was Franz Hendrickson. He stepped from the other end of the row of stalls, emerging from the darkness.

Cordelia slapped the flashlight against her thigh and it shuddered to life, flickering. "Cursed thing."

"Let me out. Mama is expecting me to help her in the kitchen," Elizabeth said, searching for an excuse. She was terrible at this... she had no courage. If they intended to murder her, which was a possibility in her mind, as it started to make sense of this, began to wrap around, she would probably lie there like a limp doll and let them stab her into oblivion.

Where was everyone else? Had no one seen them come in?

"Darling, you look frightened. You don't need to be," Franz said. "I only have a few questions, and I'm told you're the perfect little girl to help me with them."

"I'm not a little girl," Elizabeth said. Her hands turned to fists at her sides. "And if you don't want me to be frightened, stop being so frightening and let me out of here."

Darwin kept his body pressed into the barn door. "After a few questions. Not so hard."

"Your brother told me about your little trick," Cordelia said, stepping forward. She pointed the flashlight at Elizabeth, and the light was so bright against the darkness that Elizabeth's arms flew up to shield herself. Cordelia instead pointed the light beyond her. "We think you can help us."

"My brother?"

"Charles. He told us you could..." Cordelia seemed unable to finish.

"See the future," Darwin said with a flippant hand wave. "You can, yes?"

"What's it to you?" *Oh, Huck, what have you done? Why did you tell them this?*

"I'm about to make a decision that will affect the future of Hendrickson Enterprises," Franz said. His words rolled out with a softness that was not natural to him, possibly to neutralize her fears, but it only increased them. Disarming someone wasn't a tactic one used to befriend them. "I need you to tell me which way to go."

"Why would I do that?"

"Because we're family!" Darwin cried.

"Charles wouldn't have told me this unless he hoped you could be useful to us," Cordelia said. The way she moved around the room reminded Elizabeth of a slithering snake, drawing circles around its prey before striking. "Unless he was lying?"

"He was lying," Elizabeth lied.

Darwin laughed. Franz joined in. Elizabeth couldn't fathom what was funny.

"Help us, and I'll try to be nice to your brother." Cordelia curled her mouth in a sneer. "I will try not to make him miserable."

Elizabeth had seen her brother's future and didn't know that Cordelia's promise would do much, but the helplessness that had nagged at her as she watched his years unfold started to fray at the edges. What if she did help them, and Cordelia was slightly less insufferable? It wouldn't be a change to the future; only a softening of the inevitable.

"What do you want to know?" Elizabeth crossed her arms. From the corner of her eye, she watched Darwin, waiting for him to let down his guard.

"I want to know whether I should make the investment or not. Simple," Franz said.

It wasn't simple at all. Elizabeth couldn't curate her visions, or search for answers within someone's mind. She saw what she saw, and it was rarely what she'd come for. But they weren't letting her out of here without something.

Elizabeth closed her eyes. She reached a hand forward, but stopped short of making contact with Franz. She didn't want to touch him... sometimes when she did that, she saw beyond the future, to the heart of who a person was.

There was an incident... an incident so many years ago, which was the past, yes, but this incident had carried Franz into the present and would be both his future and his end.

Should she tell him?

Elizabeth opened her eyes, letting her gaze travel between the pack of carrions. Not a one of them had a conscience. Not a one of them deserved hers.

"There was a girl," Elizabeth said. "I can't see her name, but she was young. Underage. The daughter of your best friend." She bit her lip. "John. Your best friend John. Her daughter."

The smile died on Franz's face.

"You tried to woo her, but she didn't want you. You were too old for her, and she told you that, and so you pinned her down and raped her in her father's office, while the rest of the office worked outside."

"What is wrong with you, little girl? Why would make up

such a horrific story?" Darwin said. "That's not why we brought you here."

Cordelia said nothing.

"You raped her, and she told her father, which you weren't counting on. After a fight, you brought a rock down on his head and killed him. Then the young girl... Daisy, her name was Daisy, I can see it now... jumped to her death."

Franz reached out for something that wasn't there. He backed away, tried to smile, tried to speak.

"You want to know your future, Franz Hendrickson?"

Cordelia answered for him. She didn't appear to be surprised or affected by the prior outburst. "Yes, tell us."

"You'll die within the year," Elizabeth said, and her strength grew with the words, which she would not have shared with anyone less vile than this man and his brood. She should hate herself for the glee in announcing his fate, but instead found power in her gift for the first time. "Suicide."

Franz's spell broke at this. He sputtered through a series of laughs. Darwin joined in, but his were strained with fear. "Why would *I* kill myself?"

"Two reasons that I can see," Elizabeth said, and she felt herself growing, expanding, becoming larger than them all. "One, your business will fail. I can tell you what choice to make, but you'll make the opposite one anyway, because you are a selfish, vainglorious man who thinks his shit smells like roses. Two, something will finally give you cause to regret what you did to that girl and her father, and you will see yourself for the man you really are. A man who cannot live with himself."

Darwin stepped forward from the door. "This is nonsense. It's crazy. We're crazy, for thinking a stupid little girl could actually see the future."

Cordelia's thoughts traveled elsewhere for a moment. Then she nodded. "Yes, let's go. This isn't what we came here for."

Elizabeth noted that Cordelia didn't explicitly say that she didn't believe the premonition.

Franz kicked at the dust on the floor and then marched toward the door. He stopped before Elizabeth. "Tell your brother I'm on to him. You hear me? He'll pay for this trick."

Elizabeth shrugged.

"Open the door, Darwin," Cordelia commanded.

"We're going to let her get away with this?"

"She's nothing but a useless child. And I'm thirsty."

Thank God for that! Elizabeth's neck throbbed with her heavy pulse.

Darwin shoved the latch open and the doors yawned wide. "Charles will pay, though."

"You'll leave my brother alone," Elizabeth said. "Unless you want me to read your future as well."

Darwin chortled. "Sure. Right. You couldn't stand all that excellence."

"Let's go," Cordelia said as she marched ahead and outside. Both men followed. Both looked back at Elizabeth.

She smiled wide and lifted both middle fingers in the air.

MAUREEN RACED across the lawn toward Elizabeth. "What just happened? Why were you in there with them?"

Elizabeth told her.

Maureen's blood pressure soared through the roof. She drove her heels into the dewy grass and a deep groan rose from deep within her. "How dare they? Who do they think they are?"

"I told them the truth," Elizabeth said. "Franz will kill himself."

"After they threatened you!"

"They didn't actually threaten me."

"They kidnapped you!"

"I'm not sure we could call it that."

"Why do you look okay? Why aren't you more upset?"

Silent tears appeared in Elizabeth's lids. "Oh, I am upset, Maureen. But not at them."

"Then what?"

"No matter what I do, Charles is going to marry Cordelia. He's going to marry into that family."

Maureen squeezed her sister's arm. "Not if I have any say in it."

MAUREEN FOUND Charles at the river. She doubted he knew she was aware of his favorite spot, but it was hers, also, and she'd seen him go there from time to time. She kept his secret, but this was important.

"Do you know what your fiancée's family did to our sister?" she demanded.

Charles set his beer to the side. He looked around, craning his neck as if expecting she brought an entourage. "Where the fuck did you come from?"

"That's not important right now. Franz, Cordelia, and that nimrod brother kidnapped Elizabeth!"

Charles shot to the feet. "Say what?"

"You heard me." Maureen's fingers splayed out over her tiny hips. "They *kidnapped* her, Charles. Locked her in the horse barn and forced her to tell them their future."

Charles pressed his hand to his mouth and looked out over the river. Moon spilled over the surface, lighting the way for the barges. "They fucking did not. Tell me you're making this up, Maureen."

"We've already established that I have no imagination whatsoever."

His face was as red as a lobster. "What the fuck? Do they

have any *idea* what I'm capable of? What I've done?" He lifted his beer bottle from the ground and chucked it as hard as he could throw. "Is *this* why I have to marry the bitch?"

"You can murder someone later," Maureen said reasonably. "But I have a better idea."

She filled him in on everything Elizabeth told her... about the young girl, the business partner.

And then, her idea.

"You would need to help me practice. I need time. I don't... I don't even know if I could do it, you know? I've never tried, they've always just come to me, and they're all connected to me in some way."

Charles shoved his hands in his pockets and whistled out a breath, eyes closed, cheeks aflame. "And you think you could do it?"

"I said I don't know, but wouldn't that be just delicious if I could? Revenge doesn't always have to be violent."

"If not for violence, you'd be off in a nunnery."

"Listen to me, Huck. Elizabeth said this jerk Franz is going to kill himself next year. Elizabeth is *never* wrong. But she said he's a proud, boastful man who doesn't seem like the type, so something has to drive him over the edge, right? Right?"

Charles pulled his hands over the creases of his face, moaning as his hands dropped to his neck. He wrapped both hands around the soft skin there. "Let's bury this motherfucker."

THIRTEEN
THE NECKLACE

Augustus left his brother's party along with the first of the departing guests. Charles wouldn't miss him. He never wanted the party to begin with, and Augustus figured that his leaving was helping along the ushering of the end of the whole thing.

He didn't need to be in the office. It was late, and everyone would be home with their families by now... all but one. He'd also given a key to Ekatherina, which had drawn speculation and ire that he hadn't asked for and didn't need, but it did no good to explain to all the office busybodies that Ekatherina had a key because she was the only one of them who worked late and went above her duty.

Augustus would have been working, if not for the party. He would've preferred work over the event marking the beginning of the end for Charles' happiness. Augustus and Charles had never had the brotherly bond many young men enjoyed, and Augustus didn't approve of much of Charles' behavior, but he was miserable for his brother at the thought of him married to Cordelia Hendrickson. If Charles was the life of a party, she was the vacuum, sucking every last crumb of enjoyment. Augustus had hoped Charles would eventually settle down, but not like this.

He took the stairs tonight. Sometimes he still did this, to get his blood pumping harder, proof he was alive, and that he had built this. He'd never required thrills like Charles, but instead, he sought small, subtle reminders. Tonight, as he watched his older brother step into a den of lions, Augustus needed a reminder.

The office was dark, except the small light coming from the back corner. Ekatherina's green lamp was no longer the beacon on the trail to Augustus' office. The office had recently reorganized to accommodate their new growth, and the finance team had been relegated to the back, all sharing a roomy but isolated corner office. The blinds were drawn, but light peaked through the slats.

Augustus looked around at his small, but powerful empire. He was not a seven-billion-dollar man, as his brother was, but he was largely self-made. He'd started with the minimum investment needed and grown his business through grit and determination.

And, as he promised himself on the dark fall day by the river where he rescued Maddy, he'd donated half his profits the first year to the local homeless rescue.

A stack of the summer edition of Deschanel Magazine sat on the desk to his left, and he grabbed one.

He never read it cover to cover. He wouldn't have considered himself a superstitious man, but something about this nonetheless felt ominous, like if he stopped to question or assess, he would stop moving altogether. His thumb released page after page as he skimmed, but he paused when he saw a familiar face.

Spring Elopement for Rory Sullivan and Carolina Percy, read the headline under the banner *In & Out of Love.* Augustus frowned. He didn't remember approving this section, which felt trite and a small step above a gossip rag.

Carolina's beautiful golden hair flowed like a wave of amber around her tanned, glowing face. Beside her, Rory flashed the signature Sullivan tight-lipped smile. The caption read that their engagement photos had been taken after they were married, which was pointless and silly, but Augustus found himself unable to look away.

Neither looked happy, and that was two Sullivan brothers now who had married into the great potential for heartbreak. The pattern was starting off the same in the Deschanel family now, as well, and would it also continue?

Augustus tossed the magazine aside. He shifted in place, unsure of what to do with himself. Work was where he felt most himself, but his mind wasn't in it tonight, a fact both somewhat welcome and also worrisome. Much like stopping to read an article, if Augustus paused too long to question his habits, he might find the contents lacking.

His eyes were again drawn to the faint light in the corner office. Ekatherina would have heard him come in, surely, so he should at least say hello and good night, before disappearing again.

Augustus found her alone and crying. She wiped her face when she noticed him appear in the door, but he'd seen it, and she knew this.

"What's wrong?"

"Nothing," she replied. Her fingers moved with maniacal precision on the adding machine to her right.

"You're crying," he said, helpless for a better choice of words. The tears seemed so antithetical to what he knew of her. An uncomfortable anachronism.

"It's nothing."

Augustus stepped inside and closed the door. He didn't know why. It felt right. He approached her desk and sat across from her. "It's not nothing. Anything I can do?"

The whirring of her adding machine stopped, but her hand stayed hovered over the keys. He could almost see her arguing with herself. She reached for a tissue, blotted her eyes, then pulled something out of her drawer. Her hand held up a tiny cross necklace, the cross broken into two pieces.

Augustus stretched his hand to touch it, but he didn't do more than tickle the gold. "Yours?"

"It was a gift from my *mammochka*. It is all I have of her."

Augustus this time took the necklace from her hands, after a tentative nod from her, and studied the damage. The gold was of inferior quality, only plated, and the chain was flimsy and not worthy of the task. He wasn't surprised it broke, only that it hadn't sooner.

"I can fix it," Augustus said and slipped the keepsake into his pocket before she could object. Her large blue eyes blinked in surprise at his kindness.

"I do not ask this of you," she said. "You are my boss. I work hard and I pay for repair."

"I know," Augustus said. She had the money, but he knew where this money was going, and there was no way he'd let her spend it on this, not if he could help. He stood, both uncomfortable by her tears and also moved nearly to tears himself. He needed to leave, before... well, he didn't know what. But he needed to leave, and now.

"I can pay," she said again.

Augustus gestured around the office. "You already have."

He disappeared without wishing her a proper good night.

COLLEEN WRAPPED her hands around the leather steering wheel. It wasn't too late to back out of this harebrained idea. She could still change course. She could just *ask* Philip, which was what a normal person would do. He'd either tell her, or he wouldn't, but she'd have a better sense of things.

She never should have gone to see Ophelia. It wasn't that she doubted her great-aunt, but her advice was designed to never let Colleen make the mistakes herself. And because she sought it out, she couldn't very well ignore any of it. She was the instigator and the sufferer.

And then Rory, at Huck's party. This had been before all the boozing that propelled him into almost ruining his brother's life, but the words had been equally unwelcome.

"Colleen," he'd said, nudging her aside. They both knew what Carolina would think of them being alone, and both were tense from the risk. "You need to be careful."

"Excuse me?" She pulled her arm away, more rudely than she intended.

"Professor Green. Watch yourself around him. He has a reputation with his female students."

"I have no idea what you're talking about."

He'd only smiled in response, a smile that said everything. She hated him in that moment.

Philip had never given her the address to his mansion on Napoleon, but the Garden District was a small world. Tourists might refer to the more famous houses by their original names, like Magnolia Grace, but locals were more inclined to say things like, *you know, the Deschanel place on Prytania.* Colleen knew where the Green house was on Napoleon, because it was only a block from the ice cream shop where they used to walk as kids. She remembered the heavily-gabled green and tan house on the corner, looking a tad too much like something out of a Nathaniel Hawthorne novel.

Philip wouldn't be home. He was teaching classes until four, and if his version of things was to be believed, it wasn't his night at the Green house in any case. Which meant Sylvie would be there, hopefully alone. The hour was early enough that their sons should be in school, which was why Colleen had chosen to come before noon.

She had a plan. It wasn't her best plan, nor very solid even by a less-organized person's standards, but it was good enough for government work, as Rory used to say. With luck, she'd walk away more enlightened—hopefully confirming her hopes, not her fears—and at worst, Sylvie would just think she was a foolish student who made a miscalculation.

Colleen forced herself out of the car and up the steps to the round porch. Before she could knock, the door opened. A comely woman appeared, with two throw rugs, one over each arm, and she looked as surprised to see Colleen as Colleen was to see her.

Colleen didn't know if this was Sylvie or not. She realized she'd never seen a picture of the woman.

"Sorry to scare you," Colleen said and lowered her knocking hand. "I was, uh... looking for Professor Green. I'm one of his students. Is he in?"

The woman's demeanor changed in a single instant. She shifted her weight to one side and tossed the rugs on a nearby chair. "I'll just bet you are."

"He wasn't in his office, and I just had a question about an assignment."

Sylvie looked her up and down with a slow shake of the head. "I told him... I told him not to bring you sluts here. Jesus, Philip! How hard was that one thing?"

"Sorry?" Colleen's blood went cold.

Sylvie laughed. "Philip and his fucking predilections for young, smart girls. You think you're the first? Let me guess, you were first his student, then his aide and now, *miraculously*, he's free to date you because you're not a student anymore? He give you that speech yet?" Her mouth hung wide as she watched

Colleen in cruel assessment. "I told him to keep this dirty business away from my steps. Away from my house!"

Colleen wished for the moment just before she'd opened the car door. If she could just walk backward down the steps, into the past, where she could slap some sense into herself. Where she still believed Philip was just a peculiar guy, and not a terrible one.

Sylvie looked past Colleen, down the street, both sides. "You tell that no-good piece of shit that I'm done. He broke our agreement for the last time! The last time! You got that? You'll tell him?" She sneered. "I want my keys back for the loft, too. No more fucking on my dime, on my property. But hey, you look well off. I'm sure he can come mooch off you for the next twenty years. I did my time."

The door slammed in Colleen's face. She glanced helplessly at the forgotten rugs and had a strange, inexplicable urge to clean them for the woman of the man she'd been sleeping with.

Colleen had no better understanding of the Green marriage, but she had observed enough to understand her own relationship with the venerable Professor Green.

She was not the first. He had done this before, and he had his rhythm and act down to a carefully constructed science, so believable even Colleen had not seen through it until she'd already fallen for him.

This wasn't the first, or even second, time her judgment had been compromised recently. Was it this town? Her family? Her?

Or was it all of these things?

She couldn't wait a year to fix whatever inside her had fundamentally snapped. She was not herself, and there was nothing in the world that left her feeling more helpless and alone than losing the trust she had in who she was.

Colleen bent over the wheel. She gasped inward and trapped it there.

Scotland was there now, waiting. Beckoning. Promising.

FOURTEEN
THE AGREEMENT

Charles had to check twice to see if the girl next to him was breathing. She was, as it turned out. He wouldn't leave until her eyes at least fluttered open. Maybe he was a murderer, but he was also a gentleman. He shuffled back into his clothes and waited.

She rolled over to her back and her hand fell bowed in an arc above her head. She groaned as the sleep left her. "Where you going, Daddy?"

"Don't call me that." The remnants of a burned letter reformed, in the pit of his stomach. *Shelly. And my daughter.*

She grinned through her closed eyes. "You liked it last night."

"Did I?" He'd been so coked out of his brain, she might have called him the King of England and he would've cheered her on. "Home. I need to get home."

"But *why?*" she whined and let the sheet fall away, a clear temptation that wouldn't work. Once Charles lost interest, the thread snapped and could not be re-woven.

"Shit to do," he said and searched around for his wallet, which had fallen out somewhere in the throes of passion. He spotted it, bent to grab it, only for her arms to slide in from behind him.

"Don't go."

Charles hated the clingy ones. Above all else, it was a scene like this that caused him to create his one-and-done dating rules. Every now and then he met a girl who surprised him, who could handle the sex without all the extra fluffy shit, or the weirdness of the morning goodbye. Women like that were rare. Most of them married lucky men.

He wasn't in the presence of mind to deal with this one at all. He mussed the top of her head, which, even as he was doing it, felt silly and strange, and then winked at her and left.

Charles didn't know what she thought of any of that and didn't care.

CHARLES FOUND Irish Colleen roaming around the large servant's pantry near the second kitchen. She stood at the door making silent assessments, shaking her head.

"What are you doing, Ma?"

"Your sisters and I will be moving out this winter."

"Yeah, and?"

She waved her hand. "I've been spending my time, each day when the chores are done, in each room deciding what should come with us and what should stay."

"Take it all," he said. "I don't care."

"That's just foolish," Irish Colleen chided. "We'll be downsizing. Maureen, Lizzy, and I don't need much."

"Cordelia and I don't need much, either."

"You will."

"By then, all this food will be spoiled."

Irish Colleen scoffed. "I'm not taking anything from the pantry, silly boy. I'm trying to decide what to make for dinner."

"But you said—"

"Did you enjoy your party?"

"We need to talk about that." Charles wiped his palms, already greased in nervous sweat, down his trousers. "I know you don't want to tell me about Franz, but I need you to, Ma. You owe me that much."

Irish Colleen's whole body sighed. She leaned forward and retrieved a jar of pickles. "What's done is done."

"What's done is *not* done, because she's not my wife, yet, and I still have a choice."

She patted his arm. "I know you'll do the right thing."

"Mom." Charles licked his lips. His throat throbbed. "You have to tell me. You're asking a lot of me, and I'm delivering, but I won't go into this marriage not knowing." He could tell her that Franz had kidnapped Elizabeth, but what good would it do? And anyway, he and Maureen had their own revenge for that old coot.

"For Pete in the night." Irish Colleen sighed and set the jar down. "This won't make marrying her any easier, you know."

"There'll be nothing easy about marrying Cordelia no matter what."

"Fine. Very well. Grab a bottle of sherry from the top shelf, will you? And two glasses."

"JOHN HANNAFORD, Franz, and your father were the best of friends. John was a financier, and you know about Franz. His textile business was still in infancy then, but he did well from the start. He had some money he brought with him from Germany. The Hendricksons were something there, but the war changed things, he said, so he started a new life here.

"The three were inseparable for years. John was at the bedside of your father's first wife when she died, right at August's side, and Franz handled all the funeral arrangements. Franz wasn't always the ruthless man he is now. Or perhaps he was, and what happened between the three men is what brought out the devil in him. I can't say.

"You know your father was an older man when he met me. He was almost fifty by the time you came around. Of course, he never expected to become a father so late in life. Eliza was supposed to have a whole passel of children, but God had other plans for her. John was around the same age as your father, then, and Franz about a decade younger, if memory serves. But still too old for what he chose to do.

"John had this sweet daughter. Oh, what a sight she was! Name was Daisy Mae, and if she didn't look every bit of that name... Daisy's mother had died giving birth to her, and John did his best to serve both roles. He was a good father to her. A good man. When this all happened, she was about sixteen, I want to say. Still had another year or two of high school left, if that's any indication that this child was still that, a child. Certainly too young for Franz to be roaming about and messing with her.

"This was the first falling out that I recall, between your father and Franz. He told Franz to keep his hands and eyes off John's girl, and Franz told him to mind his damn business. But this was the kind of man your father was, Charles. A grown man messing with a young girl *was* his business, and he made it so. He finally went to John about it, and John flew into a rage. This was a calm man, mind you. I never saw John angry, not for long. But August told me John turned into another man altogether at the news one of his best friends was trying to woo his child. He told Franz if he didn't stay away, he'd kill him with his own bare hands. Oh, John."

Irish Colleen finished her sherry and held the glass out for Charles to pour her another. She continued on as he refilled the glass.

"I don't know if I can say this next part, but here it is, anyway.

Franz raped that poor girl. Oh, he'd say later she wanted it, but she was bloody and crying when she found her father and told him what happened. God help that poor girl, and God rest all their souls.

"To make matters worse, John found out this assault happened in his own office! Poor sweet Daisy Mae had been waiting for her father, spinning around in his chair, as *children* do, and Franz had come in, locked the door, and let the devil take him over. She'd screamed into his hand, and no one beyond heard a thing. Not one thing. Lord, I never thought... never imagined I'd have to tell this story ever again."

Charles reached across the table and covered his mother's shaking hand. "You're doing fine."

"John... I suppose you can imagine how John reacted. He flew into a rage. He called August and said he was going to confront Franz and would appreciate some backup, but he was going even if he had to go alone. August was all the way out here, an hour away, but he said he'd come... I've wondered, so many times, if only he'd been closer. How things would have turned out differently. How very differently.

"When August got to Franz's, the deed was done. John was lying in a pool of blood in the back garden, with Franz pacing back and forth before his body. Franz said it was self-defense, but your father couldn't find any sign of a weapon. Franz had always been the weakest of the three, weak in character and in all other ways. The bloody rock discarded by a nearby tree. This is where it all went wrong for your father. He should have called the police and ended it there. Sent Franz away. I was pregnant with you at the time, over six months, and when he told me later about everything that came next, I had such great pains that I thought I was losing you. And I told your father, we could have taken Daisy Mae in and given her a life. It didn't have to be this way.

"Franz convinced your father to help him, and I know your father regretted this to his dying day."

And beyond, thought Charles with a shiver.

"They put John into his car and drove him out of town, along the river, searching for a levee break. When they found one, they piled bricks on John's gas pedal and sent his car, with him inside, right into the Mississippi. They found him two days later, because the front of the car got stuck somewhere in the bank. Police investigations weren't what they are today, and no one questioned how the front of poor John's head was missing. No one questioned it. Your father, who could convince anyone of anything, just like your brother, Augustus, saw to that. John's death was ruled a suicide. And two days later, poor Daisy Mae, well, she jumped from the bridge near where her daddy had gone in, and she was gone, too."

Irish Colleen crossed herself. She used her arm to brush away the tears.

Charles felt the puzzle pieces coming together. His father's words to Maureen.... Elizabeth's choppy revelations to Franz. Perhaps his father wasn't the stand-up man Charles always believed him to be, but unlike Charles, who had taken several lives with his own hands, August was guilty only of making a bad decision to help a friend. Surely Charles hadn't gotten his murderous tendencies from his father... and if not him, then from who?

"What does this have to do with me marrying Cordelia?"

"They made a pact," Irish Colleen said. "August never said this, because he wouldn't want to upset me when my job was to keep you safe until you were born, but I suspected he feared Franz would kill him, too, if he hadn't gone along with helping. You see, the only thing that could guarantee your father wouldn't say a word to anyone was his complicity. Once John was in the river, Franz told him that if he said anything, Franz had August's fingerprints on the rock, too. He'd moved it, after all, at Franz's beckoning. August realized too late that Franz had been playing him the whole time. And then Franz made him swear that their firstborn son and daughter would marry, binding the families, and their secret, for life. That this was the only way to guarantee the secret would stay a secret."

"That's some medieval shit," Charles said. "Why did Dad agree to that?"

"I asked him the same thing. I thought of my child, of you, in my belly, and I hated your father for deciding your future for you. But the children are not the product of the sins of their fathers, and August helped me see that."

"But why does it matter now? Dad is dead. Franz can't hurt him."

"Dead men's reputations still matter, Charles. *You* carry his reputation in you, in the honor of the heir to the kingdom of New Orleans. Do you really want this case re-opened? Your family dragged through the mud? We could lose everything."

"They can't send us to prison for something Dad did."

"I'm not talking about prison. You think you'll be the darling still, if people believe you're the son of the man who murdered John Hannaford and drove his sweet Daisy Mae to fling herself from the Sunshine Bridge? People still say her ghost haunts there."

"People say a lot of dumb shit," Charles said. He couldn't believe this... that he was hostage to the machinations of the man who had harmed a child, killed his best friend, paralyzed his mother by fear, bribed his other best friend, and then got away with it?

No. Franz would not get away with any of this. The worst of the lot, and he was still out there, doing as he pleased, enjoying the spoils.

"I'm going to talk to him," Charles said.

Irish Colleen's hand shot across the table. "No! Don't you dare, Charles. I trusted you with this, because you're right, you deserve to know. But I won't have you rocking this boat! As long as that man lives, we have no choice but to live up to your father's end of the pact! Don't you see? It's the only way."

No, thought Charles. *Not the only way.*

AUGUSTUS WAS NERVOUS. He couldn't say for sure what had prompted him to stand forward as the hero of this tale and fix Ekatherina's necklace. He'd done it without thinking, and now he had it, sitting upon his knee as he drove home in tortured silence.

He wasn't himself then, nor was he now, as he held the new and improved cross tight in his fist, standing outside the finance office.

Augustus paid the jeweler double to expedite the service. He couldn't bear to face Ekatherina again, knowing he was the only thing standing between her and her mother's heirloom.

He hoped he hadn't done too much. Afraid it would break again, this time he'd had the whole thing coated in fourteen-karat gold, and as an extra touch, one he was beginning to regret, he'd added in several tiny emeralds, the birthstone of both Ekatherina and her mother. He wasn't supposed to know that, and she might hate him for it.

Ekatherina took the repaired necklace in her hands. Her eyes marveled, a hint of moisture giving them a luminescent quality.

"Your birthstone." His voice cracked. "I hope that's all right."

"This is too much," she protested. Tears forged a wet path over her porcelain cheeks to her brilliant smile. She clutched the cross in her hand, the way a child would hold a beloved toy. "You do too much."

"You don't like it?"

"Like it?" Ekatherina's eyes closed as she brought the cross to her chest. "I love it. I am in your debt."

"No," Augustus said quickly. "You're not. I didn't do this to make you feel like you owed me anything. I did it because I knew I could help you. I wanted to."

"Why?"

Why. Augustus had been asking himself this very thing. The necklace was only the most recent thing to cause him to put his own feelings and behaviors into question, but it started when she'd come through those doors with her worn clothing and serious, determined face.

"I want to help you and your family, Ekatherina." Who was speaking? It wasn't him... it was another man, the man, perhaps, he should have been.

Her smile faded. Eyes narrowed. "I'm saving money. I can do it."

"But I can do it faster." He didn't know anything about romance. Nothing about sensitivity, or the subtle language of love. He'd failed both in loving and in not hurting Carolina, and he didn't know what he was feeling now, but he pushed him and his words forward, despite his deep reservations. "Marry me, and I'll do anything for you."

Ekatherina's hands fell to her lap. "What did you say?"

Take it back. Tell her you shouldn't have said it, or pretend she heard you wrong. This is madness, pure madness. You hardly know her! You're not the marrying type. She doesn't love you.

"Marry me. Marry me, Ekatherina" he repeated, louder, with more confidence. When she gaped at him with her shocked face, he added, "Maybe I'm not what you pictured for a husband?"

Ekatherina's head shook. "No, it is not that."

"Then what?"

"You don't love me," she said. "And I am broken."

"When I see you, I don't see someone who's broken. I see

someone whose spirit is bigger than anything that tries to bring it down," Augustus said. "You deserve everything in this world, Ekatherina. I'm not... I'm not a romantic man. I can't give you that. But I can keep you safe and secure, and I can and will bring your family here. You have my word."

"I say no," Ekatherina said. "Because you regret."

"I won't regret it," Augustus insisted.

She shook her head. "I do this myself. And when I marry, I do for love."

I do love you, he tried to say, but didn't know if the words lodged in this throat because they weren't true, or because they were.

"Good night, Ekatherina," he said and left.

FIFTEEN
THE WALK

Evangeline found out about Augustus' proposal to Ekatherina by accident.

She opened a piece of mail addressed to him, but only because it looked like junk and it was her job to sort the real mail from the advertisements. It was no advertisement, though. She turned the letter over in her hands, which was in fact a bill, and the amount owed sent her eyes flying wide.

Evangeline waited for him to get home and jumped from her seat in anticipation when the door opened and closed.

"Four thousand dollars at Brennan's Jewelers? What the hell, Aggie?"

Augustus looked perturbed at the immediate assault. He set his briefcase aside and took his time hanging his coat before her took the paper from her. "Why are you opening my mail?"

"I didn't know what it was!"

"That's not an answer."

"I thought it was garbage. You know, junk mail. I always check first, to be sure."

"Didn't see the jewelry store on the return address line?"

"I did, but... why would you be buying jewelry? I thought they were sending you a flier."

Augustus tucked the bill inside his blazer. "You should be sleeping. Don't you have a seven a.m. class?"

"So that's it? You're going to deflect, so you don't have to tell me?" Under her breath, she added, "Never cared about my bedtime before."

Augustus heaved a great sigh. "There's nothing to tell. I may have asked Ekatherina to marry me, and she may have said no, and so now we move on."

Evangeline stopped breathing. The revelation was the last thing she expected, though now that she considered it, what else could it have been? "No."

"No? That's what you have to say to me telling you I might be getting married?"

"You're not marrying her."

Augustus pulled his shoulders back. "Not up to you, Evie. You've made your feelings about Ekatherina known. I don't need to hear them repeated."

"But she said no! What are you gonna do, tie her down and hold a gun to her head while she says her vows?"

He sighed again. "I won't dignify that with an answer."

"But why her, Aggie? You could have anyone in the world, anyone!"

"That's not how life works, Evangeline. If it did, our brother would be marrying Catherine instead of Cordelia. And if you really wanna know? I've never met anyone else I wanted. Not Carolina. No one."

"It doesn't mean you won't!" she cried. She was desperate to get through to him, before he, too, made a great mistake. It was hard enough watching Charles prepare to throw his life away. But not Augustus. Not him.

He threw his arms out. His jacket came up. "Look at me,

Evie? What do I have to offer anyone? Money? I don't want a woman who is only looking for that, and yet what can I give a woman who wants more? Ekatherina is... well, she's like me. She knows who she is, and she'll do what she needs to in order to get by. Who else do you know like that?"

Evangeline pressed her lips tight and didn't answer him. He was right, but he was also very wrong, and she didn't know what to say.

Augustus lowered his arms, and when he clenched one of his hands, Evangeline could see it was trembling. "I don't know why I'm this way, but I am, and it won't change. Maybe I could be happy, too. Maybe there's someone right in front of me who won't need more than I can give, and we can be happy together."

"Aggie..."

"If you can't support me on this, then say nothing," he said and climbed the stairs.

EVANGELINE CALLED COLLEEN. There was no *way* Colleen would let Augustus go through with this, and she'd have better words and better ideas to get through to him. Evangeline wanted him to be happy, but not like this. He was selling himself short, and there was a woman out there worthy of Augustus Deschanel, but her name was not Ekatherina Vasilyeva.

But Colleen was a mess herself. She'd discovered the professor was precisely the man Ophelia implied he was, and rather than being angry at him for the deception, she was woefully disappointed in herself.

"I've let myself down. I've let the family down. What good am I to anyone like this?"

"You're feeling sorry for yourself," Evangeline said. "As you should. He's an asshole, Leena. You deserved better than that."

"I'm not, though. I'm not sorry for myself, I'm... *angry* at myself. My judgment is compromised, and I can't be trusted."

Evangeline rolled her eyes. When Colleen was in self-loathing mode, no logic would pull her back out of it. "We can commiserate on this one later, I promise, but we have a big problem that needs our attention *now*."

"He hasn't even called me, Evie. Not once. He could have cleared all this up, with just a phone call."

"You know why he hasn't called, Leena."

"I compromised my personal values for this man, thinking I could trust him and who we were together. I did... I did *cocaine* for this man."

Evangeline's bushy brows shot up. "We're definitely coming back to that. But right now I need you to come talk to Augustus about this Russian situation."

"He's living his life," Colleen said, and that's when Evangeline knew this conversation was a lost cause.

"Sorry about Philip. I can bring over beers tomorrow if you want."

"Sure. Maybe."

"I'm going for a walk. Night."

"A walk? It's past midnight!" Colleen repeated as Evangeline cradled the phone.

Evangeline chuckled a bit to herself that she could still be a surprise to others. They each had their roles to play in this family, and Evangeline's had never involved physical fitness. She was born with limited energy, and as she aged, she preserved it the way one might save a fine wine for a special occasion.

She wasn't walking for her health, though. Not physical, anyway.

Evangeline loved science because it gave her more than an explanation. It approached the world with boundaries, and as long as there were boundaries, you were safe. Water was two parts hydrogen, and one part oxygen, and that was true regardless of the weather, the time in history, the time of day. The world around her hummed to a precise and largely unchangeable set of calculations.

That, she could understand.

The burning sadness in her heart she understood less, because it seemingly had no boundaries. No edges... no end. She pretended to be okay, because she supposed that was what others around her needed. She had a physics teacher who said that intelligent people did not always possess strong emotional intelligence *because* of this expectation that emotions should behave in the same ways as the fixed rules and theorems of science. What he didn't say was how to overcome this.

She liked to imagine that one day she'd wake up and the things that had happened to her would hurt no longer. She'd smile at the sun coming through the curtains, stretch her hands over her head, and have an amazing day.

But this was the problem with being smart. Evangeline knew better. And so she walked, every night, when the cicadas sang softer, and the evening breeze cut through the humidity enough to send the scents of the Garden District into a curling perfume for the senses.

Even the safest neighborhood in New Orleans wasn't precisely safe in the middle of the night, so she'd tucked Augustus' Smith and Wesson Model 19 into the back band of her jeans. She didn't know why he had the gun; she'd stumbled upon it by accident, and he certainly never mentioned having one. Evangeline would be surprised if he knew how to handle it. But she did... one of her only productive takeaways from the Dauphine crew. A friend of Ethan's, Dalton, had some family land out by Riverbend, and they would go shoot at bottles and cans. Ethan sometimes aimed his pistol at a bird, and the girls would scream until he stopped. Evangeline wondered if he did this to make the girls scream, or if he really did want to shoot birds but didn't want his groupies to see him for the monster he was.

This was a serious gun. Police issue, she thought, from her limited knowledge of such things. The commitment in owning such a gun made Augustus' motives even more curious to her, but she would never ask him. He was a man of his swirling secrets.

Evangeline had a few paths she took. Sometimes she would meander up and down the fifty or so square blocks that made up the Lower Garden District. Other times she'd walk the length of Prytania from where Magnolia Grace sat at Eighth, west until she saw Touro Infirmary, and then, if she really needed out of her head, all the way until she hit Audubon Park. She considered that a dead-end for Prytania, even though it continued on for a few more blocks beyond the park, before hitting the river.

Then there were the nights she wanted to be closer to the pulse of the world, and she'd jump up a few blocks to St. Charles Avenue, which slowed but never slept. The mechanical hum of the streetcar was as soothing to her as a mother's voice to others, and she skipped along the neutral ground, in the grass between the east and west tracks, hands deep in her pockets. Sometimes, if the streetcar was empty when it passed by a stop, she'd jump on and ride it from Carondelet to Carrolton until someone else hopped on, breaking the anachronistic spell of her pull to the loudness of silence.

Tonight was quieter than usual. The students from Tulane and Loyola, who lived peppered throughout the smaller apartments of St. Charles that were squished between the assuming Greek Revival, Italianate, and Victorian mansions that held court, were asleep, with early morning classes awaiting them.

Evangeline closed her eyes as the streetcar from the west ambled by. It was a slow, lumbering beast, but enough to send a soft breeze passing over her, and this always calmed her. When the machine was gone, she opened her eyes, and, startled, saw someone else walking.

She rarely encountered another person walking in the middle of the night. She'd be amongst a plethora of drunks and die-hards if she were doing this in the Quarter, but not here. Evangeline squinted—she needed glasses, but was holding out as long as she could—and saw it was a young woman, around her age.

The woman, on the south side of the avenue, stopped as well and waved. She tugged at something, and Evangeline saw she had a small dog on a leash. Evangeline hoped that little yippy thing wasn't her protection, because a mild wind would punt that thing ten blocks to the river.

Evangeline checked both ways and then jogged away from the neutral ground and across the street.

"I don't normally see a lot of people out this time of night," she said, by way of introduction.

The girl threw her long blond hair over one shoulder. It covered half her pale blue tube top, which she filled out nicely. The hand not walking the dog was shoved deep in the pocket of her miniskirt. "I like the quiet."

"Yeah? Me too."

The girl pulled her hand from her pocket and held it out. "I'm Amnesty."

Evangeline took it. "No shit?"

"No shit."

"Cool name."

"Yeah. Yours?"

"Evangeline."

"That's a cool name, too."

Evangeline shrugged. "Named for my Catholic grandmother, whom I've never once met."

"So, you live around here?"

Evangeline was suddenly embarrassed to say she lived in

Magnolia Grace, one of the most photographed homes in the Garden District. So she said, "Yeah, on Prytania. You?"

Amnesty seemed taken aback by the reciprocal question for a brief second. "Here, on St. Charles."

"Do you normally walk at night?"

Amnesty shook her head. Her gold hoops bobbed in her ears. "No, but it seemed nice. You know?"

Evangeline nodded. "It is nice. Feels like the city is mine alone this time of night."

Amnesty smiled and threw her head back. "Ours now."

"Oh. Yeah, ours."

"I'm headed back home. Walk with me?" Amnesty looped her arm through Evangeline's without waiting for an answer.

Evangeline spun with Amnesty, returning the way she'd come. She still had some walk in her, but this was strangely more interesting. More alluring.

"Do you go to school?" Evangeline asked.

Amnesty shook her head. "I take care of my sick grandfather. It's just the two of us in that big house. When he dies, I'll be all alone there."

"Where are your parents?"

"They died in a crash when I was little."

"I'm so sorry."

Amnesty shrugged, and Evangeline saw how soft and pale her shoulders were. She had the strange urge to cup her hands over them and feel the down against her palm.

"And you, Evangeline? What's your story?"

Despite her inexplicable inclination to tell this young woman everything, Evangeline held back. "I live with my brother right now, while I'm going to school."

"You have a big family?"

"Seven... I mean six siblings."

Amnesty marveled at this. "I can't imagine. Do you love it?"

"I suppose."

"It's nice to be alone, too. No one to tell you what to do, or how to do it. There's so much freedom in living your life."

"What about your grandfather?"

"Oh, him? He doesn't know anything about me."

"You don't feel like your life is on hold, caring for him?"

Amnesty shook her head. "Only if you think college is the single path for a person. I don't. We get one life, Evangeline. I want to feel every single moment, and I never forget it could be the last thing I feel."

What a strange answer, thought Evangeline.

"This is me." Amnesty stopped in front of a set of tall wrought iron gates. Beyond, only glimpses of the mansion could be seen behind the carefully planted flora. "Tomorrow, then?"

"What?"

"We'll walk again."

"Sure. I mean yes."

Amnesty's smile lit up the night around her. She poked her head forward and kissed Evangeline square on the mouth before unlatching the gate and disappearing beyond.

Evangeline didn't move for another minute. Her hand hovered over her mouth, not quite landing.

She waited for the familiar sound of a door closing, to make sure Amnesty was inside safely, but when it didn't come, likely masked by the heaviness of the plants guarding the home, Evangeline made her way back down St. Charles toward home.

Amnesty. A strange girl with a strange name. But no, strange wasn't the word Evangeline was playing with in her mind.

Free.

Amnesty was an unusual girl, like she'd been dropped in from Narnia or some other far off place.

Evangeline smiled in the dark, cool air, relieved to know this wasn't the last time their paths would cross.

WINTER 1973

VACHERIE, LOUISIANA
NEW ORLEANS, LOUISIANA

SIXTEEN
THE ATTEMPT

Maureen had a special disdain for libraries. When she was younger, they were touted as some magical place, where one could disappear into foreign worlds, love stories, adventures, and anything else one might be in the mood for. All Maureen found in a library was a sea of things beyond her reach and potential.

No one knew why she couldn't focus. Worse, no one cared. They chalked it up to an over-taxed mind that refused to settle. Sometimes she was called lazy. But Maureen was neither of those things, and the lack of definition on her problems only made them more frustrating.

Great Expectations had been the first book she'd ever been able to make it even halfway through, and she didn't know why Miss Havisham had grabbed her attention so soundly. Or why she'd both loved and loathed the perfectly devious Estella, who she fancied herself after in her more darker moments.

But her love of one book did not make her a bookworm any more than eating pizza made her Italian.

Yet, if she was to find her usefulness in this family again, she must push past her annoyance. She had half a mind to go back to Charles and tell him he should kill the Hendrickson patriarch after all, but if Elizabeth's visions were true, and they always were, then the man would die next year by his own hand, which seemed a more poetic victory. In the meantime, he must suffer for what he did to Elizabeth, and for the future Charles had signed up for, for reasons no one bothered to explain.

Maureen had all but promised Charles she could do this, when she had no idea at all if that were true. One of her greatest resentments over being a necromancer was that she knew ultimately *nothing* about it. She knew none of the rules... none of the limitations. She had no means to control it; to enflame or subdue the strength of it. At times, she wanted nothing more than to be truly alone, but there were others when she enjoyed talking to her father, or Maddy. Sometimes she even enjoyed taunting Mr. Evers.

At no point had she *ever* summoned the dead. Every single one of her specters came of their own will, or whatever they possessed in the afterlife. She didn't ask for them. She didn't invite them.

So how, now, was she going to invite the dead Daisy Mae Hannaford to come talk to her?

Chelsea Sullivan, who was not quite the innocent thing she wanted everyone to believe, once told her about these books she checked out from the public library. *You can't get them at the school,* she'd said, and then explained she'd been promptly grounded for having them in her room. *There's a whole world out there, girls. Witchcraft! Love spells! Summoning demons! You have no idea!*

Maureen wanted to wipe the ingratiating smile right off Chelsea's face by giving her a full accounting of what the Deschanels could do without checking out damn books from the library, but she had learned enough from Elizabeth's bullying what *not* to say to her peers. Besides, Chelsea knew about the Deschanels. Most of the Sullivans did.

She didn't have the faintest idea where to find books like this, though, and suspected that asking the librarian might yield a call to Irish Colleen. So she wandered the aisles for almost an hour before she found the section entitled *Occult*. There wasn't much to it... no more than a dozen books... and she almost missed it altogether.

Maureen waddled to a private table in the back of the library with her precariously stacked eleven books, every last one of the *Occult* titles. They all had fancy, gothic titles, like *Necromancy at Midnight* and *An Encyclopaedia of Twelfth Century Practices of Samhain*. What was the difference, she wondered, as she opened the first tome, between a witch in these books and what she was? Was she more of a witch, because she was born one? Or were these women, who had poured centuries of knowledge onto pages for posterity, who had earned their place, the ultimate of all witches?

Most of what she read sounded like a bunch of bullshit. *Swirl together the eye of a crone and belladonna, and burn incense at the full moon.* Right. She didn't know any crones whose eyes she felt like taking, and that sounded like far too much work for a 'maybe.'

The last book she opened, which was smaller and the cover less flashy, caught her attention. It was a diary of a woman named Hopestill Wolfe. The foreword of the book, written by the publisher who found the diary, said that Hopestill, or Hope to her family, had been a mild-mannered and subservient housewife to Obadiah Wolfe, a blacksmith and farmer, in the late 1700's Appalachia. No one knew, exactly, where they had lived, except that it had been in a small community, far from any big town, and that when they moved there, their fortunes took a downturn due to Obadiah's inability to find work. They'd moved from Williamsburg, Virginia, due to unknown circumstances and came north, to what was believed to be what is now Upstate New York. One by one, the seven Wolfe children began to die of unexplained, mysterious deaths, and after the loss of the third, after prayer failed, Hopestill was believed to have fallen in with some of the native mountain women who practiced a different brand of faith. The publisher called this witchcraft.

Seven children, thought Maureen. This had to be a sign.

Maureen spent the rest of the afternoon reading about the tribulations of Hopestill Wolfe. Hopestill was not like the witches they learned about in school, cunning women who could not be trusted and whom you never wanted to turn your back on. Of course, Maureen always knew that was untrue, as witches were everyday women in her world, but that ancient fear pervaded and became a modern one. Even today, the world was inhospitable to magic.

The cunning women of Appalachia were part Celt, part Cherokee, a mix of settlers and centuries-old natives. According to Hopestill, they were feared and reviled, but when prayer failed, they were also sought out, for their powerful healing. After Hopestill's third child passed, a daughter named Grace, Hopestill ventured into the mountains to find these women.

From them, Hopestill learned powerful wards, which the women told her were needed to fend off the demons plaguing the Wolfe household. Demons, they said, were drawn to the weakness in man, and Obadiah had done something terrible, and this terrible thing had brought them to the mountains. The diary never said what that terrible thing was, and Maureen was so connected to Hopestill, as she had been to Miss Havisham, that she forgot why she'd come to the library to begin with and found herself powerfully disappointed.

But the women taught Hopestill something else, as well.

Hopestill mourned for her three lost children and was compelled, several times, to attempt her own life to be with them.

When the Appalachian witches learned of this, they comforted her with a secret they had shared with very few: The dead never truly died. They were here with them, always, for those who had eyes to see.

These women were not born with magic, but had been born *to* it. From both the Celts and the Cherokee, they had mixed their knowledge into something united and very powerful, and they were not afraid of what it wrought. They showed Hopestill their deepest secrets, which was both a blessing and a curse. For once Hopestill learned how to see and speak with her lost children, she was never the same again.

Maureen had to go back and read a couple dozen pages, for the reference to *how* Hopestill accomplished this was so brief she'd missed it. She wondered, was that a rule of these mountain witches? That their magic could be passed by mouth alone?

She found it when she went back and made notes in her journal. *Every person among the dead has a tether to their living life. You must find it. A physical item, different for all, but this is the link. It may be something they left behind, or something that speaks their truth.* There was nothing else but this, no notes about the magic or the ceremony required. But Maureen realized she might not need anything else. She already had the magic. She only needed the link.

Maureen closed the book. She set the other ten books on the cart for the librarian to re-sort—oh, how she wished to be a fly on the wall when they saw this strange selection and tried to suss out the reasons!—but hesitated to set *The Appalachian Diary of Hopestill Wolfe* down with them. Maureen had only made it halfway through the woman's story, and she had to know how it ended. She looked both ways and then slid the thin book up under her shirt, and then swung her handbag over the front before rushing outside, blood and heart pumping.

ELIZABETH THREW her dolls in the large box. She enjoyed the sound they made as they whipped through the air and landed in a heap, all higgledy-piggledy, nothing like the neat row they'd formed above her head for so many years. She smiled when she heard the distinct crack of porcelain as one broke.

"Your therapist might have something to say about the way you're treating those dolls," Connor remarked. He folded clothes into neat piles in another box.

"I don't have a therapist."

"It was a joke. Lighten up."

"I'm not feeling funny right now."

"Well, you look funny."

When Elizabeth didn't laugh at this either, Connor set his box aside and walked over to her. "What's wrong, Lizzy? Are you sad about leaving here?"

She shook her head. "I never liked it here. It was nice to be away from the kids in my old schools, but... no, I won't miss it here."

"Something's wrong," he said. "If you don't know by now you can tell me anything..."

Elizabeth dropped the last of the wretched dolls in the box. "The next two years are going to be terrible for my family, and us moving is just the beginning. I should have known better... I guess, I should have known that we could never be happy for long. Not us. Not the Deschanels, not—"

Her words were cut off by a kiss. Elizabeth gasped and at the last moment stopped herself from moving away. Connor pulled back and then did it again, this time parting her lips with his tongue, which was slimy and weird and wonderful.

A burst of life rolled to the surface from deep within her. It cried out for more.

Connor stepped back. He wiped the back of his hand over his mouth. "Don't be mad."

"I'm not mad," she said and could barely hear herself over the intensity of her heartbeat.

"Want me to do it again?" The question was eager, but also tentative.

"Yes," Elizabeth said.

IRISH COLLEEN WAS busy packing when Maureen made it back to the house. She snuck quietly in, before she could get roped into the same chores. She had to practice! The sooner she mastered this skill, the sooner she could come to Charles, hat in hand, ready to reap their revenge.

Maureen didn't dare risk trying to summon another Deschanel. She suspected those closest to you were the ones that stayed, and she already had a whole tribe of family ghosts she'd as soon be rid of. So she thought hard about an alternative.

The answer came quicker than she expected, because it was a story she'd never forgotten.

Ten years before, a woman on a neighboring plantation had been murdered by her husband. Salvatore Guenard had run his wife Constance over with a piece of equipment from the farm, and when the police arrived, he hadn't even bothered with an excuse. Maureen still remembered the headline: *Yeah, you bet I did it. And I'd kill the bitch twice, God willing.*

Salvatore was serving a life sentence in Angola, and the property fell into disrepair. Guenard Plantation had been in his family for over a hundred years, so there was no bank to claim it, and no family, either. The estate had enough funds to pay the taxes for two hundred years. And so there it sat, in limbo, belonging to no one, exactly.

Maureen drove by the place every time she went to New Orleans. The house still looked all right, with only a few vines snaking up around the bottom of the columns, but without regular maintenance, the land was overgrown. Maureen remembered hearing that the police hadn't taken anything with them, and so everything—including the infamous tractor—was still exactly where Salvatore had left it.

Maureen knew nothing about Constance, but she thought, perhaps, she might not need to. What if her link, her thing left behind, was the very thing that had taken her life? If it was still there... it couldn't hurt to at least try.

With Hopestill's diary tucked into the back of her jeans, Maureen emerged from her car after parking it behind the old house. She didn't want to risk someone driving by and noticing that someone was lurking around a house that had been empty for a decade.

She wished she'd worn something more suitable than her platform heels. As she stepped through the chest-high grass and wheat and whatever else now grew wild here, her feet connected with one piece of debris after another. Who knew what was out here?

Past the curing shed, she saw it: the tractor. Someone, probably the police, had tried to cover it at some point, but the plastic shroud hung flapping in the wind, stuck on a piece of metal.

"Here goes nothing," Maureen said. She touched the book of her new friend for good luck.

"Constance Guenard... if you're here, I wanna talk to you. I'm not here to harm you... not like that bastard Salvatore." Maureen winced. Bashing her husband might not be the best tactic. Maybe Constance had died not knowing what happened to her?

Maureen ran her hands over the rusted metal. The key was still in the ignition. If she turned it, would it start? "Constance... this is weird for me, too. But I can talk to the dead, and if you have something to say, why not talk to me?"

A chill passed over the back of Maureen's neck, and she turned to see a woman she recognized from the papers.

"Hi, Constance."

"What's happening? How is this happening?" Constance shielded her eyes from the sun, as if that, or anything, could harm her.

"I'm Maureen," Maureen explained. "And I have no idea why I can talk to the dead, sorry. But I can, so feel like chatting?"

"How long... have I..."

"Ten years."

"Ten..." Constance breathed out and a sob caught in her spectral chest. "Ten years. He took so much from me, that son-of-a-bitch. When I'd given him so much... *saved* this property from ruin, with my family's fortune. And then he stole it. All of it."

Well, this was progress. "So you remember?"

"Oh, yes."

"You'll be happy to know he's never getting out of the clink, then."

Constance's eyes darted around, unsure where to land. "Oh, yes."

Maureen smiled. "Any messages you want me to pass off to your man in Angola?"

Constance turned. "Oh, *yes*."

SEVENTEEN
THE COMPROMISE

Colleen hadn't been back to campus since her fated meeting with Professor Green's wife. Thinking back, perhaps she'd intentionally chosen the last day of the term, or at least subconsciously. Somewhere, somehow, she'd known what she'd find, and returning to classes after would have been impossible.

Her winter term was negligible, anyhow. She'd finished enough credits in her third year to graduate early, but Colleen didn't know who she was if she wasn't a human being set in constant, perpetual learning, and so instead of graduating early she'd drug it out as long as possible. In order to continue on through spring, she'd had to settle for only one class per term, a decision her guidance counselor told her, more than once, was *patently pointless*.

Colleen tried to explain to him that she couldn't ever let herself be idle, but he'd only stared at her as if she'd begun to grow a second head while they were talking. He searched for ways to help her finish quicker, while she sought any possible way to prolong the inevitable. He didn't understand her any more than she understood him.

She arrived to class early, as she always did, and was the first student in the lecture hall. But she wasn't alone.

The professor sat at her desk looking flustered. Two men in suits flanked the desk. One checked their watch just as Colleen entered.

"Miss. Deschanel." Professor Caan stood. Colleen knew her, because she'd taken one of her literature classes her second year. Colleen liked her, and the defensive waves coming off the woman set her immediately on high alert.

"We'll take it from here," the man on the left, the watch-checker said.

"Colleen," Professor Caan said. She stopped whatever she was going to say next and shook her head. "Best of luck to you. In everything."

"Miss. Deschanel, will you come with us?" the other man asked. He flicked at some lint on his suit, which was too heavy for New Orleans, even in winter.

"What's this about?" she asked. She clutched her purse tight against her side and shifted into defensive stance without realizing.

They must have sensed her tone, for the one on the left introduced himself as Mr. Dickinson, and then introduced his colleague as Mr. Sellers. "Everything's fine. We'd love some of your time. It won't take long."

"I have class."

They exchanged looks. "Don't worry about that."

"I'll ask again, what's this about?" She knew those names, Dickinson and Sellers, but from where?

Mr. Sellers put a hand on her arm and gently turned her toward the door. "Let's go back to my office."

"Who are you?"

"As I said, this is Mr.—"

"No, who *are* you?"

"They're from the board," Professor Caan blurted out with a guilty, but victorious look.

"The board," Colleen said, and then some of the story started to come together.

"My office would be a better place for this," Mr. Sellers urged, with a warning look to the professor.

Two more students entered the lecture hall. They paused at the serious situation unfolding.

"My office," he repeated.

"Yeah, sure," Colleen said, but rid herself of his arm and walked ahead of them.

SHE KNEW what this was about. Of course she did... what else could it be? Colleen Deschanel, model student, from the family who provided one of the largest annual endowments to the educational institution. She couldn't guess where this was going, but suspected the journey there would be like walking on broken glass.

"What is the nature of your relationship with Professor Green?" Sellers asked, before she'd even had a chance to settle into her chair.

Colleen saw no reason to lie. She wouldn't be here if they didn't already know the answer. "We were sleeping together." She cleared her throat. "This didn't start until after I was no longer his student."

Dickinson scribbled notes in his leather notebook.

"And you were aware of the code of conduct relating to students and teachers, were you not?"

"Have you had this conversation with Professor Green?"

"Just answer the question."

"I'm aware that the onus and accountability for such an action falls solely on the teacher, not the student."

Dickinson's pen slid furiously across the page.

"Are you suggesting you are not accountable for the decision to take your relationship with Professor Green to a more personal level?" Sellers watched her closely.

"I'm suggesting he was no longer my professor, and that when I expressed concern with the arrangement, he assured me the rules no longer applied if I wasn't his student."

Dickinson raised a brow and continued writing.

"You are aware, I assume, that the responsibility for understanding the rules of this university are yours and that the blame cannot be transferred to another?"

"Why is this coming up? Why now?"

"A third party made us aware of the situation."

"A third party?"

"The wife of Professor Green, who, as you might imagine, is quite beside herself at the betrayal."

Colleen wanted to roll her eyes so badly. Philip's wife wasn't upset about the affair, only that he'd had the bad form to bring it to the family home. "Why are we here, gentlemen? I'm not denying I had an affair, however short-lived, with Professor Green. It's over now, and I'm glad for it. But he's not my professor, and I'm graduating in the spring, so what's the point of this?"

Dickinson tapped his pen against the pad.

"We're graduating you now, actually," Sellers said with a slow drawl. He opened a folder on his deck. Inside was a thick, official document. Colleen didn't dare draw her eyes there. "We're gifting you the remaining twelve credits, for your exemplary scholastic achievements, and allowing you to leave Tulane with your bachelor's degree today."

Colleen tried hard not to gasp. "You're kicking me out."

"No! No... of course not, Miss Deschanel. You are, of course, one of our most treasured students, and one cannot be defined by a single mistake. But we deemed it best that you not be on the same campus as Professor Green, under the circumstances."

"I'm sorry, you're kicking me out, and he gets to stay?" Colleen gripped the wooden arms of the chairs so hard she felt the skin break.

Dickinson pretended to write.

"We thought this would be an amenable compromise to you both. Professor Green has a long and reputable history here and has reached his tenure. We didn't want this black mark to mar his career any more than we wanted it to jeopardize your future. Why, just today we heard you'll be attending the University of Edinburgh in the fall. How wonderful!"

Colleen blinked away the dark spots threatening to send her into oblivion. This could not be happening... there was no way... it was impossible... not to her.

"You're bribing me to walk away."

"No, Miss Deschanel—"

"You know who I am... right?"

"Yes, of course, we're honored you chose Tulane for your studies, and that your family continues to patronize us."

"So you know how much money we donate each year."

Sellers went silent. Dickinson closed his notebook and ended the farce.

"Miss Deschanel, we're giving you two terms off. Most students would be thrilled."

"Most students don't work as hard as I do. Most students aren't as dedicated and haven't given as much of their lives to this place as I have!"

"This is a token of our appreciation for that. We felt punitive action would be too harsh for someone of your caliber, and we hoped you would be happy with our decision."

Colleen rocketed forward out of her chair. She struggled to

breathe, and if she didn't get out of there, now, she'd scream or faint or something completely and wholly unacceptable.

"You understand our dilemma. With Green's tenure and all," Dickinson said, his sole contribution to the discussion, which earned him a hard glare from Sellers.

"Oh, yes. You're counting on my obedience. It wouldn't do to lose a great *male* professor, or my generous donations." She reached forward and snatched the folder from the desk. "There will come a time where you both regret this."

"Colleen—"

"No, you were right before, when you called me Miss Deschanel. And one day, you'll be sitting across from me, and I'll be the one telling you what *you're* going to do, and *you will remember this.*"

IT WASN'T until she was free and clear of the drab building that Colleen released the breath trapped in her chest. She pitched forward, heaving out the air in her lungs as if it were poisonous... the emotion rolled forward, outward, until the gasps turned to sobs.

EIGHTEEN
THE ASSAULT

Maureen didn't ask how Charles had come upon the clothing of Daisy Mae and John Hannaford. *These are the shirts they were wearing when they both died. Best I can do,* he said, and she almost laughed at how short he sold this. If this was going to work, he couldn't have found anything better to bring her. She imagined him bribing the police and quickly stopped herself from going too far down that rabbit hole. With Charles, knowing was being complicit, and she had enough of her own skeletons to last a lifetime, thank you very much.

Daisy Mae's shirt was a yellow sweater, the kind Maureen was forced to wear when she was still in bobby socks and pin-curled hair. The wool was thick and distorted, like when you accidentally put it through the washing machine, but that made sense with how she'd died. John's shirt was another matter. She couldn't tell what color it had been before Franz took the rock to him, but it was a dark, faded copper red now, thick and hard in the heavier spots.

She didn't want her hands on either of these things, but as far as she knew, that was part of the deal here. Constance Guenard hadn't appeared until Maureen ran her hands over the rusted and derelict tractor that had killed her.

What if she was wrong? What if Constance was a fluke? How would she know?

Practicing summoning Daisy Mae was out of the question, because it was likely this was a one-shot deal, and she wasn't taking any chances. Once Constance spoke her piece, she said she was going to be getting on. To where, she didn't say, but when Maureen tried to get her back, she was gone. For real gone.

Maureen pummeled her fist into her thigh. Oh, there was so much she didn't know! What if Daisy Mae and her father were for real gone, too? How did someone even *do* that? Why were her ghosts not forever gone? Were they lost?

Hell's bells!

Maureen buckled and unbuckled her seatbelt. The metallic clicks lulled her, kept her calm. Charles was supposed to give her the signal. Once Franz's last guest left, they would knock on the door to the townhouse and deliver their message.

An engine started nearby. She strained to see, but Charles had parked the car around the corner and given explicit instructions not to leave the car until and unless he gave her the signal. The sound roared to life then ebbed as it faded into the distance.

One flash of light. Then two.

Maureen grinned and pushed hard on the heavy door of her brother's Trans Am.

FRANZ LET them in with no more resistance than a glare of mild annoyance. He waved Charles in and assessed Maureen with an expression that gave away the fact he didn't remember meeting her before, though they'd been introduced twice.

"Is this one of your girlfriends, Charles?" the man quipped. "I'd hoped you'd exercise better discretion."

"My sister," Charles grunted. "I know she's about the right age for you, but you even try it, you're a dead man."

Franz scoffed at this, but his eye stayed on Maureen a moment longer than she was comfortable with. He wasn't terrible to look at, honestly, but one couldn't forget he was a murdering rapist who'd kidnapped her sister and exploited her.

"What is it? It's past ten," Franz said. For the first time he seemed to be coming around to the realization that the visit was not a typical one.

"Maureen has something she'd like to show you. Isn't that right, Maureen?"

"Show me something? What is this, show and tell?" He rolled his watch forward on his wrist and made a point of checking it, despite the clocks positioned all around the room. "Charles, I don't know what you're playing at here, but I'm not interested. It's been a long day, and I have an early meeting tomorrow."

Charles nodded at Maureen. Her hands shook as she withdrew Daisy Mae's shirt.

"What? What is that?" Franz asked.

Maureen closed her eyes. She whispered the name of the dead girl aloud, which elicited an audible gasp from Franz, and then waited.

The silence in the room was deafening. Her pulse throbbed as the seconds ticked, and nothing happened.

One.

Two.

Three.

Four.

Fi—

Maureen passed out.

IT ALL HAPPENED SO FAST. Maureen was alert and focused in one moment and the next she was flying back through the air in a soft arc. Charles' instincts threw him forward to catch her before she could hit the ground. Her light weight bowed his arms, and he had an irrational but powerful fear that she might be dead, and if so, it would be his fault.

Her body rocked forward as a gasp overtook her. She struggled for breath and clawed at her face and hair, eyes darting around the room like a wild animal who'd awakened to find itself in a cage. She ripped loose of his arms and crouched low on the ground, poised to attack.

Neither Charles nor Franz moved. Charles didn't breathe.

The tension released from Maureen's limbs and she fell back onto the carpet. "Where am I?"

"Maureen? Are you okay?" Charles hovered before her in midair, afraid to touch her.

"Maureen? Who's Maureen?"

Franz crossed his arms. "I don't know what devilry you two are up to—"

"Mr. Hendrickson?" Maureen rolled forward onto her hands and lifted herself up. "What's going on? Where are we?" She turned around and looked up at Charles. "Who's he?"

"Maureen?" Charles circled around his sister. He stood at Franz's side, united in their growing confusion. "What's wrong?"

"Why do you keep calling me Maureen?"

"Well, shit, Maureen, what should I call you, then?" Charles asked.

"Most people call me Daisy Mae, so I don't see why you would do any different."

"We're done here," Franz said, with a note of authority undermined by the squeak of a cracking voice. "Get out."

"Maureen..." Charles warned, but couldn't decide what he

wanted her to stop doing. Was this an act? It didn't seem like it. What it seemed like was that his sister was gone and someone else had taken her place. She didn't wink or give him any indications this was part of the plan. Although she wore the face of his sister, something had shifted just beneath the surface, and it was enough to make her seem like a complete stranger.

Daisy Mae turned to Franz. "I'm... well, I'm waking up now. I was confused for a moment, but I'm not so confused now. I shouldn't be here."

"You're damn right," Franz said. He was frozen in place.

"I shouldn't be here, but here I am," Daisy Mae continued. She lifted Maureen's arms and inspected them, turning her hands over. Flexing. "I'm not myself."

"Stop it!" Franz pointed at Charles. "Make her stop."

Charles threw his hands up, helpless.

"Will this last?" she asked Charles.

"I don't even know what this is," he said. His chest tightened. His control over the situation had slipped away with whatever had happened to Maureen. The unknown chewed at his guts. What if he couldn't reverse this? What if this dead girl never left? Even if he could convince her to pretend to be Maureen, no one would believe it. One family dinner was all it would take for the whole thing to come crashing down.

Irish Colleen would murder him.

"Bullshit," Franz said, but now his voice lacked the earlier vigor.

"Maybe I don't have much time," Daisy Mae mused. "Maybe God has given me this gift."

"You aren't from God," charged Franz.

"I'm not from wherever you come from, either," Daisy Mae said. "People like you don't go to the place people like me came from. I thought I'd never see you again, Mr. Hendrickson, and unfortunately I was wrong about that, but there must be a reason

I'm standing here in front of you again, after all these years. How many has it been?"

"I'm not playing your games."

"Twenty-three or so," Charles answered as he swallowed down a growing lump at the back of his throat. "That's my age, anyway, and I wasn't born yet, but I was on the way."

"So I'd be almost forty," Daisy Mae said. She offered a sad smile, which looked foreign and strange played out on the face of his sister. Charles could now see her for who she was beyond the physical form she now possessed. "I don't feel that old. I still feel just as I did when I died, only... different."

Daisy Mae regarded her host's hands once more before clasping them together. "I'm here for a reason, it seems, and my father taught me never to waste the gifts given to us." She turned to Franz. "Remember that thing you used to call me, when you thought no one else was looking? Not even my father knew. Your little dandelion. When you pressed my face into my father's desk, you told me you were plucking my petals, one by one. Did you ever pay for your crime?"

"What the fuck," Charles whispered, running his palm over his lips.

Franz's face was a mask of white terror.

"I guess I should be more specific, Mr. Hendrickson. Did you ever serve even a day for raping me and then murdering my father?"

Franz was a stone statue. The only sign of life was the bobbing of his Adam's apple.

"No, of course you didn't. My father knew who you were. He knew you were lily-livered. A coward with no loyalties and no morals stronger than your desires. You're no better than an animal, are you? It's like you never evolved into a full man. You're missing pieces."

"That's not how it happened," Franz choked. "You were attracted to me... you said—"

"Tell me, what did I say that made you nearly strangle me to death as you had your way?"

"I can't remember, but you wanted it. I know you did."

"I never wanted it. I never wanted *you*. What I wanted was to graduate high school and go to college in California. I wanted to design buildings. I wanted to get married and have children, and watch them grow up. I wanted to paint in my spare time, and I was pretty good at it, you know? I wanted to learn ballroom dancing, and my father even signed us up for a class, but we never went because you raped me, and then when he did what any father would do, you killed him."

"You don't know what you're talking about."

"She does," Charles said. He stepped forward. "You killed John Hannaford and then bribed my father into helping you cover it up. You ruined two lives, and then you ruined his, and now you want to ruin mine by making me marry into your terrible fucking murderous family so you can continue to skate by without any consequence."

Daisy Mae regarded Charles with a curious smile. "I remember your father. You look so much like him. He was a good man."

"I'm sorry he helped prevent this monster from being punished. I'm so sorry."

She touched his arm. "Mr. Deschanel did what he needed to do to protect his family, just as my father did. Mr. Hendrickson does what he needs to protect himself."

"This isn't real... you're..." Franz stammered.

"Your little dandelion?" she finished. "I was never that. I was never your anything. And do you know why I killed myself?"

"You loved your father," he offered weakly.

"I killed myself because he had you listed as my guardian in case of his death, and I couldn't bear even a minute in your hands."

"Jesus Christ," Charles whispered. "Why?"

"I'll give you one guess."

Charles glared at Franz. "You sick shit. *You* convinced him to unknowingly prostitute his own daughter, and then you killed him. You were always planning to kill him."

Franz ignored him. "I never meant for your father to get hurt. He said he wanted to talk, but then he went insane!"

"I wonder why," said Daisy Mae.

"It was self-defense!" Franz cried.

"Ahh," she said. "So that's how you sleep at night. But I know something no one among the living knows."

"What?"

"What really happened."

Franz searched for something to do with his hands. He reached first for the nearby chair, but it was too far, and then he looped them behind his back. With a grunt, he moved them to his pockets. "No one was there. No one except John and me."

"And where do you think John is now, Mr. Hendrickson?"

Franz's mouth flapped in helpless pursuit of words.

Daisy Mae laughed. "Did you think I was going to actually tell you where the dead go? No, you're not worthy of such privileged information. But I've seen my father. He was the first thing I knew after the darkness took over, and he couldn't believe I was there, too. He was so sad, and so furious, because he knew why I'd done it. Before I moved on, he told me what happened in that house. How you first denied what you did to me, and then taunted him, *laughing*, claiming he was a terrible father who couldn't even keep track of his daughter. He demanded you turn yourself in, Mr. Hendrickson, and when he wouldn't take no for an answer, you waited for him to turn around, and then, like the coward you are, you hit him from behind with the rock."

Franz stopped trying to talk. He listened to her, visibly deflating with every word she spoke.

"You hit him again and again. And when he rolled over, hands before his face, in surrender, you brought the rock down against the front of his face and delivered the death blow. You looked him dead in the eyes as you killed him. So, you're wrong, Mr. Hendrickson. I know what happened. Now Mr. Deschanel's son knows what happened. And what's most important of all is, *you* know that even if you never see a day in prison, you raped a young girl who couldn't defend herself, and then took her father's life while his back was turned, like a cravenly pig." Daisy Mae put her hand to her mouth and covered a smile. "Yes, thank you, Maureen, for this gift. I've said what I came to say. Mr. Hendrickson knows what he must do now."

MAUREEN AWOKE in her brother's arms. Her head throbbed with the worst headache of her life, worse than any hangover she'd ever had. She used Charles to right herself and then stepped away.

"Do not fuck with my family, Hendrickson! You hear me? There's fucking more where that came from!" Charles was yelling.

"It's all lies!"

"Fuck you and your little dandelion bullshit!"

"I don't know what happened... are we ready to try?" Maureen swayed on her feet.

Franz and Charles were both white as ghosts.

"What?"

"We already did it. It's done."

"What are you talking about? I passed out."

"Daisy Mae was here... she was in you," Charles said.

"In me?"

"She spoke through you."

Maureen looked at Franz, as if he would be of any help at all. His head shook, not at her, not at anything. He was there, but he wasn't.

She looked at the clock. The time read 10:27. They'd arrived at 10:10. "No... really? She really spoke through me? You're not making this up?" But they weren't. Their faces said far more than their words.

"I think we're done here," Charles said.

Maureen had so many questions! This was huge... a huge, *huge* step forward in understanding who she was and what she was capable of. She'd only just learned she could summon the dead, and now they could speak through her. There were so many possibilities she could hardly stand it!

"What are you going to do?" Franz asked, and the fear in his voice, in his eyes, reduced him to an even lesser man than the one they knew him to be already.

"Me?" Charles snickered. "Nothing. Not a damn thing. I did what I came to do."

Maureen, hands on hips, nodded, though she remembered none of the lashing Franz had taken.

"Which was?"

"Lizzy said you're going to kill yourself. If Lizzy says something, it always comes true. Always," Maureen said.

Charles looped an arm around her waist and winked at Franz. "We just helped you figure out the 'why.'"

Maureen held back her inappropriate laughter until she was safely in the passenger seat of Charles' car.

"Holy shit! You have to tell me everything!"

But Charles didn't share her enthusiasm. He wrapped his

fists around the wheel and then pressed his forehead to the worn leather.

"What? It was successful, right? He saw her? He believed?"

"You could say that."

"Then what's the matter?"

"Don't you understand? Lizzy said he'd kill himself next year, but she also said I was going to marry Cordelia. If both things are true, then he doesn't off himself quickly enough to save me from a future with that terrible hag."

Maureen's smile faded. She considered what kind of comfort Charles might want and decided he wanted none at all. "He still deserves to die, Charles."

"I almost killed him with my bare hands tonight."

"But you didn't, because Lizzy said—"

"Just *once* I wish Lizzy had the good sense to lie."

"Maybe Cordelia will die in a tragic car accident on your wedding night, before you have to fuck her."

Charles lifted his head and smirked in the dark car. "Only you would have the balls to say that aloud."

"And you."

He nodded. "And me. All right, buckle up. I'll take you home."

Maureen's heart sank. Home meant something different to each of them now. For him, from now on, it would be Ophélie, looming dark and large and lonely until his family filled it and either fixed this or made it worse. As for her, she had a new home, back in New Orleans. She'd wanted to come back so badly, but now that she *was* back, she only felt the hollow longing for the things she'd learned about herself at Ophélie.

"I don't like how separated the family is now," she said as the car angled out onto the uneven cobblestones. "Augustus and Evangeline at Magnolia Grace. Colleen leaving for Scotland. You..."

"It was gonna happen eventually." He smiled from his peripheral. "Unless in your crazy head you had it that we would all live with Mama for the rest of our lives like a bunch of degenerates?"

Maureen grinned into her lap. "No, I guess not."

"No. Most of us are grown now. Time to live our lives." He didn't sound very convincing.

"Still."

Charles stopped at the light. He turned to her, one hand on the wheel, one on the gearshift. "Maureen, you can call me any time. Day or night. I'll drop whatever I'm doing and come to you, if you need me."

"Nah, I'll be fine."

"I'm serious." The light turned green, but he didn't move. "Tell me you understand."

A car behind them honked.

"Are you gonna go?"

"Not until you say you understand."

"Hell's bells, go already!"

"Then tell me you'll call me before trying anything dumb again."

The car honked again, this time drawing out the sound. "Fine, fine!"

"Promise it."

"I promise!"

"Good." Charles threw the car into gear and took off. "I've kept your secret. I did try to use it on Cordelia to scare her away, but it didn't work, and she thought I was full of shit."

"I believe you."

"That thing with Franz and Daisy Mae, it was your idea. I wouldn't have suggested it..."

"I know, Huck. It was *my* idea. And I'm glad we did it, if it gets that cretin Franz off the planet before he can hurt other girls, or murder anyone else."

"I hate to tell you this, but there's no fucking doubt in my mind he didn't stop with Daisy Mae. She probably wasn't his first, either. Men like that don't get a taste and feel satisfied."

Maureen chewed her lip as she watched the houses fly by. "I was thinking that, too."

"Are you okay? That possession didn't fry your brains or anything, right?"

"I don't think so. I feel okay. Just wish I remembered it."

Charles nodded. "I hope you know how useful that could be to you in life. Not every problem can be disposed of in the Maurepas swamp."

Maureen looked at him.

"What I'm saying is, these gifts, we have them for a reason." Charles pointed his cigarette at her. "You have this gift for a reason. And it's not to continue late night gab fests with Maddy, God rest her soul, if you get my drift."

"I think so."

"You're a Deschanel. Your list of enemies will have as many digits as your bank account. Not all of them will go away quietly."

"I know."

"Good. Good, it's good you know, Maureen, because I think things just get harder from here. For all of us."

EVANGELINE RUBBED HER SHOULDERS, which were sore from spending the day helping her mother and Elizabeth unpack. Maureen should have been there, but she was off doing God-knows-what, not wasting any time getting back into her old bad habits now that she was in New Orleans again.

So much had changed. The seven, now the six, were scattered like fractured chunks of what they once were. She supposed this was part of growing up, but it didn't feel like that. Charles was alone now at Ophélie, which she knew felt more like a prison than a promise of the future ahead. Although she lived with Augustus, she never saw him, unless she was lucky enough to catch him as he was coming or going. She was almost never at the office anymore. He didn't need her, if he ever had, and she harbored so much resentment and rage for the Russian—she refused to call her by her name—that this only got in the way and added tensions to the office.

Evangeline wasn't yet ready to process Colleen leaving for Scotland, so she didn't.

At least her mother and younger sisters were close again. The townhouse was only a couple miles away, just a streetcar ride and quick walk away. Or a *hop, skip, and a jump,* as their father used to say.

She still heard his voice sometimes. There were moments when it was like he had never left at all, and others where he was as foreign to her as a stranger. Evangeline had adored her father, and she feared he never knew how much. She was neither the loudest nor the neediest of his seven children, often lurking behind in the shadows. Did he love her as much as he loved the others? Sometimes what hurt more than losing him was never having answers to her questions.

The bed called to her aching body. How she longed to throw herself into the plush covers, falling diagonally, fully dressed. No one was there to nag her about switching into her pajamas... that was one of the few real perks of being an adult, as she saw it.

But if she did that, she'd be letting someone down.

Evangeline didn't have a number for Amnesty, and besides, it was too late to ring someone's house. They'd met every night for weeks, and every time Evangeline thought she was too tired, or didn't need a walk, she thought of Amnesty and her curious blue eyes and soft face. She never let herself think too much into any of this, and as long as she kept her thoughts skimming the surface, she had no reason to fear them.

She slinked past Augustus' room, but she needn't have bothered. He was still at the office, and why not? So was the Russian.

Evangeline flew down the stairs and out the door before she could change her mind.

NINETEEN
THE ANSWER

Colleen didn't belong anywhere.

Irish Colleen and the younger girls were in New Orleans now, settling into their new townhouse, blocks from the Faubourg Marigny. Instead of moving her stuff to the room her mother set aside for her, Colleen had thrown all her boxes except the essentials into storage.

Irish Colleen raised a brow at this decision, but said nothing about it. She never did. She wasn't the kind of mother who fussed over such things as her children's emotional well-being. A pulse, an education, and a lack of trouble were her expectations, and Colleen had those in spades.

The essentials fit into two suitcases, which Colleen imagined herself carrying between Ophélie, the New Orleans townhouse, and Magnolia Grace, crashing from night to night as she awaited her inevitable exodus across the ocean.

That's what it was now to her, an exodus. An escape from everything. Herself, her choices. Her town, her home, and even her family. This last one hurt almost as much as the doubt she'd created in herself. All her life she'd told herself that everything she must do for her own life must also serve her family. Service to one's family was next to service to God, and some, like her, were called to this in far more important ways. She believed this not because anyone had told her so. To the contrary, Irish Colleen had informed her, in many ways, that her sense of duty was overblown, if not misplaced. But the bar to lead this family was high. Ophelia was a matriarchal goddess, and when she was gone, someone had to step in who could operate at her level. Charles wasn't ever going to be that person, and Augustus had no appetite for anything resembling a front seat on affairs. There was no way Colleen would let that honor go to Blanche's line, even though there were several worthy candidates, like Eugenia, or even Pierce. No, this honor must return to the heir's line, where it belonged, and if her brothers wouldn't step up, Colleen had to.

She had no choice. She'd given up so much in homage to this belief.

Except she wasn't at all sure about any of this anymore. If Colleen could not even see through the trite cliché of the professor seducing his student with false words and intentions, then how could she be trusted to make significant decisions on behalf of her entire family? She was disgusted with her actions... with her lack of instincts strong enough to overcome her inflated ego and burgeoning libido. She hated Philip almost as much as she hated herself. But, still, at night, she thought of him, and of the fire he'd ignited in her that she first thought did not exist and later with him, believed could never die.

Her list of failures lined the shelves of her mind's compartments, blurring the boundaries, knocking down the walls built to protect herself from plumbing the depths of her self-realization.

Colleen counted them down, as she did almost daily, in her moments of self-reflection before she once again closed the doors.

She should have known her father was sick with cancer. She could have blown past Irish Colleen's need to respect his wishes and saved him, so he'd still be here, alive, today, and so much else wouldn't have gone so horribly wrong. All of their misfortune started with the wasted death of a great man.

Had she tried harder to reach Charles, he wouldn't be stumbling through life but instead taking charge of it.

If she'd been more patient with Madeline and tried to understand her plight without judgment, she'd still be here, trying to save the world.

If she'd been a better sister, a more understanding one, a better example, she could've headed off the situation with Maureen's teacher before it ended with turning their big brother into a murderer, a role he seemed in no hurry to turn away from, and she'd even gently encouraged.

And to further insult her attentiveness, this hadn't been enough for her to mind Maureen, who continued to struggle and then ended up pregnant, and being forced into an abortion that broke her spirit. She'd failed her middle sister not once, but twice.

She'd pushed Evangeline's needs aside for her own and ignored her cries for help, and then her sweet Evangeline sought comfort among people who eventually caused her great, irreversible harm.

She couldn't forget Elizabeth, who had suffered all these years, unable to control her gift or her tongue, and Colleen's influence and intervention could have saved her many, many years of grief.

She'd let herself fall for her best friend, only to break Rory's heart, not once but many times, and as a result, skewing her own view of what love should mean, and whether she was even worthy of it.

And all this culminated in her fateful affair with Professor Green, and her fall from grace with Tulane.

Wounding her further was the phone call she'd received from Rory. Their first child was due the following summer. She should be happy for them, especially after Carolina's tragic, hush-hush miscarriage months prior. Colleen had pushed the two of them together, and now they were doing exactly what she'd said she wanted, which was to make a life. But now that they were, she couldn't stop the ache deep in her chest, even by plying it with logic. She and Rory were not meant to be. She knew it. Ophelia said it.

Still, it burned.

Failure to love him. Failure to let him go.

Colleen had come to a decision. Although she wasn't due in Edinburgh until late July, she would leave New Orleans just after Christmas. She wanted to leave now, but Christmas would always and forever be non-negotiable in this family, because of the ways in which it pulled them together with the memory of Madeline. She couldn't believe three years had passed. Three years since her beautiful, passionate sister had flown through the halls with her dreams and desires that were too big for any of them.

"What are you doing in here? Alone? In the dark?"

Colleen squinted through darkness at Evangeline as she stepped through the front door of Magnolia Grace. "You know me. Overthinking everything."

"Everything?"

"All of it. My whole life."

"Ah, yes. Your specialty." Evangeline closed the door and switched on a soft lamp on the desk. "You staying here tonight?"

"I think so."

"You know I love having you here, and Augustus probably wouldn't know you were here even if you told him, but don't you think you should pick a place and, I don't know, move in? You're not really the transient squatter type. More like the perpetually neurotic type."

Colleen ran her hands over her knees. Her vision blurred, losing focus. "I just need to get through the next few weeks."

"What does that mean?" Evangeline leaped through the air and bounced into the cushion next to Colleen's. Colleen grunted at the invasion, then wondered if that, too, was a failure. To be human. To connect. To relax.

"Christmas is in two weeks. Sometime in January, I'll be leaving for Edinburgh."

"What? That soon?"

Colleen nodded. "Something is fundamentally *wrong* with me, Evie. I'm not myself, and I'm not anyone I recognize, and I'm certainly not anyone I'd want to know."

"Leena, what is this self-hating bullshit?" Evangeline leaned forward and wrapped Colleen's hands in hers. "Seriously, why are we brooding alone in the dark? We both know you're not a failure, and that there's nothing wrong with you. Nothing *much,* anyway."

"You say that because your expectations of me are different than the ones I hold for myself."

Evangeline rolled her eyes so hard they fluttered. "*That's* an understatement."

"Ophelia won't be around forever. She talks about it like she's already decided I'm next in line."

"If you're surprised by that, you're the only one."

"But I have failed everyone. I failed you, too."

"Oh, like hell, Colleen. You couldn't fail me if you worked at it."

"You know I did."

"If you're talking about the rape, I'd rather we didn't."

"I'm sorry."

"Don't be sorry. Just don't make it your cross, too, because I can't bear knowing you suffer from it, too."

"See?" Colleen said. "I can't even be supportive without making it about myself."

"At worst, you're a bit of a narcissist," Evangeline said with a slow nod. "But what I see is a big sister who does more for her family than any sibling on the planet. I see my best friend, who makes mistakes but then learns from them. Who are we without our terrible mistakes? Boring, that's who."

"You're my heart, Evie. But I need to leave for a while. I have to get my head on straight."

"Yeah. You do."

Colleen gave a slight smile. "So now you agree with me?"

Evangeline dropped her hands and threw them up in surrender. "Hey, I never said anything was wrong with you! But if you think so, that's what matters, right? You're not gonna listen to a damn thing I say. Or anyone says. You never did, even when they were right. *Especially* when they were right."

Colleen's grin turned whole.

"You ask me all the time what I need. I need my big sister to stop hating herself. I need her to see how much good she does in the world, and how big her heart is. And if she needs to go off and fuck William Wallace and his woad-faced rebels for a few years, well..."

Colleen punched her. "You're so crude."

"You love it."

"Maybe."

"I don't know if I can do this," Colleen admitted. "Isn't that sad? I profess to the world that I'm capable of anything, and I can't even overcome the homesickness before it happens."

Evangeline chuckled. "Why do you think I haven't gone to MIT yet?"

"That's not why."

"It's part of it. I'm positively terrified of leaving New

Orleans! What if people in Massachusetts don't know how important I am?"

Colleen laughed. "You'll let them know, in your own very special way."

"Mostly for Aggie." Evangeline answered the rest of her own question. "I worry about him, and that Russian."

Colleen patted her arm. "He couldn't have anyone better in his corner if he is in trouble."

"You're really not concerned about him?"

"I think, of all of us, Augustus deserves to be happy, and he's smart enough to know what he wants."

Evangeline frowned, visibly deciding whether to continue down that path. "Want me to come with you to Scotland? Help you get set up in your new digs?"

"Only if it won't interfere with school."

"Fuck school."

"Evangeline!"

"Really, Colleen. The more I think about it, you should go. You've carried the family on your shoulders all these years and, you know, I think I can do it for a while. I can take over. Call me Atlas." Evangeline flexed her upper back.

"Thanks for saying that." Colleen exhaled. "That's what's eating at me, that there's a task I'll be leaving behind. Maybe it is narcissism, because I can't help but believe everything will fall apart when I leave."

Evangeline shook her head. "What do you think the most important trait in a leader is? Here's a hint: it's not leadership. Every last one of our politicians are narcissists, and probably sociopaths, too, but let's ignore that for now, because that's not my point. Only those bold, and let's face it, a touch delusional enough to believe they're capable and worthy will step up to lead. And you're going to lead this family one day, Colleen, just as Ophelia does now. You'll probably do it better. And you know what? You'll do it with heart and conscience, and both of those are bigger than any delusions of grandeur you might secretly harbor about your importance."

A well of powerful emotion rose within Colleen and she rolled forward into her sister's arms. Sobs shook her body and she didn't try to stop the tears like she normally would. Tears were weakness, and only those without the proper mettle cried—this she had told herself, all these years, and now she knew she was wrong, wrong. There was a time and place for tears, and to let others be strong for you when you were at your lowest.

She was not weak.

She was wounded.

But she would emerge stronger.

Just like the motto on the Deschanel family crest: The strong shall rise again.

And she *would* rise again.

"It will be okay, Leena. I promise," Evangeline said, and for the first time, Colleen believed these words when spoken by another.

AUGUSTUS WAS the only one in the office when the clock struck twelve. He was anxious. Every night, they had a ritual. A routine. Around eleven, twelve at the very latest, he would gather his things, switch off his light, lock his office. He'd see the small beacon of light from the corner office and wait a few moments, until that, too, switched off.

Ekatherina would emerge, jacket either draped over her arm, or, if the weather was cooler, over her shoulders. She clutched her worn purse in both hands in front of her. A tight, polite smile was her acknowledgment, and from there they would descend the stairs—never the elevator, except those two weeks when her ankle was troubling her—in united, comfortable silence, until they stepped out into the midnight air. There, she would say, *Have a good night, Mr. Deschanel,* to which he'd reply, *You, too, Ekatherina.*

There was little to no deviation in their ritual, and Augustus knew it was as important to her as it was to him, for she performed her role with great precision. Even when he had something more to say, he'd save it for the following day, where it could be given its own importance, separate of their nighttime dance of choreographed steps and scripted words.

Nothing had changed after his failed attempt to woo her as his wife. She was more reticent toward him in the office, but at night, she was his, and he hers, for the few short minutes it took to complete their ritual. Some things were bigger than ego, or emotion.

He'd told her, almost in passing so as not to give it too much weight, that he'd renewed her VISA another two years. She quietly thanked him, and he moved on, as if this was not the biggest thing anyone had ever done for her.

Where was she tonight? She'd left at some point when the office was still a bustle of activity, slipping out without him noticing. She never left early, or on time for that matter. Ekatherina, like Augustus, staked her survival on knowing where she was meant to be at all times and living her life accordingly.

Was she okay? Was she sick? It was too late to call; that window had passed, and he didn't want to leave her with the impression that she was not allowed to take sick leave. If anyone in the office had earned some time off, it was her.

There was yet work to be done. When was there not? But this disruption to what was normal, what was comfortable, was more than his focus could bear, so Augustus began to walk through his side of the ritual. He first gathered his things, and then, crossing the small office, went to switch off the light.

He gasped. He wasn't alone.

"Mr. Deschanel, I did not mean to scare you."

"Are you all right, Ekatherina?" Adding to his worry about her earlier departure, standing before him now she looked pale and drawn. Her eyes were red, as if she'd been crying.

She looked at her hands, which worked around a small object. "I meet problem after problem. I have money. They say they want this amount and I give them, but it's not enough."

"Who is they?"

"The Soviet government. They say money no longer buy visa. They shut down all requests. They shut down my family."

Augustus rolled the leather handle of his briefcase over his fingers. "What do they want?"

"They do not say. And I am so alone here, Mr. Deschanel. I come here, feeling so brave, and I know now I am not so brave." Tears rolled down her cheeks. "I am scared, and I have no one."

He shifted the briefcase so both hands had something to do. He feared if he didn't, he'd do something untoward, like touch her, or God forbid, pull her into an embrace, as the strange urge within him pressed him to do. "How can I help?"

Ekatherina's hands blossomed, revealing the object: the gray velvet box from Brennan's. "You tell me when I say no to marry you that I sell this for money to help my family. But I cannot, Mr. Deschanel. You buy this for me. You care what happen to me."

Augustus cleared his throat. "I care very much, Ekatherina."

"I try to sell, but I cannot. Just as *Mammochka*'s locket has meaning, so does this ring. You buy for me, Mr. Deschanel. You want to give me a life that is not lonely, where I am not scared anymore."

He nodded, speechless.

"I no want your money." Ekatherina shook her head, as though afraid of the words trying to come out. "I no want you to marry me for any reason but love."

"I... you know I'm not like the other young men, with words

and flowers. But I love you in my own way, Ekatherina, and if that's enough, then I'll give you everything I have to give, without ever asking anything from you in return."

"You do love me." It was not a question.

Augustus nodded. "Yes."

"Not like other men."

"I'm not like other men, and neither is the way I love."

It was her turn to nod. "I know nothing about romance. What good is that when people starve? When my family starve? I know no romance. I need no romance. You can't give. I can't give either."

Augustus dropped his briefcase. It slipped straight from his hands, and he took hers in his, the ring box pressed between them. "You were meant to come here, Ekatherina. I believe this, and I don't put much into the idea of fate. But I know you were meant to come here, and I was meant to... to love you. Do you believe that?"

"I begin to believe many things now."

Augustus withdrew his hand, and with it, the ring box. His hand trembled, fumbling through opening it. There was a proper way to do this. He should just give it to her, let her put it on herself. She didn't need the proposal. She might not even want it. But he feared their marriage would be a series of him calculating his failures to be enough for her, and he would not start things off wrong.

He lowered into a kneel, but his sport coat button was fastened and he had to stop to fix this before continuing. Her smile at this was playful and put him at ease, though his heart beat so fast and so hard his breath hitched.

"Well, then. Will you marry me, Ekatherina?"

"Da."

The ring slipped. His fingers and palms were oil slick, and he struggled for purchase. At last he had it and he placed it around her tiny finger. It was a touch too large for her, and he promised to have it sized right away.

He asked her if she would like to come home with him tonight, and she said yes, though he sensed her hesitation and quickly wished he could rescind the question.

When they stepped into the vast and quiet emptiness of Magnolia Grace, Augustus was, for the first time, ashamed of his wealth. Ekatherina had pulled herself from the dregs of a life that was killing her, to work herself near to death. He had so much, and she, so little.

Augustus worked because he chose to. And as much as his pride refused to let him slow down and live off the fat of his family, he was forced to admit this house had been an endowment. He'd done no more than be born the second son of the most prominent man in New Orleans.

And he knew, as she gaped like a starving child standing before a feast, he knew, he knew, he *knew* that he would give her every last bit of what he had to see her smile and mean it.

"I'll show you to the guest room," he said and pretended not to see the subtle flash of relief pass over her face.

TWENTY
I'M GIVING IT BACK

It was Christmas Eve, and the family was scattered.

There'd been a huge family fight about where Christmas should be held. Irish Colleen insisted Ophélie was the center of the household, but Charles put his foot down. He said if the house was his, then he'd as soon turn it into a mausoleum than subject his family to the bad energies coming. Evangeline didn't know what the hell he was talking about, and suspected he didn't, either, but it was obvious to everyone how depressed he'd become.

The townhouse was plenty big enough for a family holiday, but Irish Colleen was self-conscious about serving from her small kitchen and condensed dining room. She tried to ask Augustus how he felt about Magnolia Grace, but he hadn't returned her calls, and they wondered if he even knew it was Christmastime.

Only Evangeline knew what was really on his mind.

"You should break the news on Christmas," she said days before she'd marched into his office demanding to know why *she* had been staying at the house. And then he told her, and she couldn't believe it. She could, and she couldn't, and it was all too much.

"I'll share the news when I'm ready," he said, and he didn't look nearly as happy as a man newly engaged should. This quelled her temper. Some.

"When are you marrying her?"

"We haven't decided, but it won't be a big affair. We may go down to the courthouse. After the New Year." He lifted his pen as he moved from page to page of his stack of papers, looking for places to sign.

"You're acting like this isn't a big deal," she charged.

Augustus looked up. "I can't win with you. Either she's terrible for me, or I'm not thrilled enough to be marrying her. Which is it, Evangeline? Pick one. Or neither. Please."

"Why is your future wife sleeping in the guest room?"

"That's none of your business."

"I don't understand you."

"You never did."

"Don't say that like it's a personal failure of mine," Evangeline said. Her cheeks grew hot. "It's not. Maddy didn't understand you, either."

Augustus' hand froze in mid-signature. He clenched his jaw. Then returned to signing.

"I'm sorry," she said, more quietly. "I didn't mean that."

"You did. It's okay. I prefer honesty to platitudes."

"You know I love you, Aggie."

"Then don't add to my stress by giving me trouble about Ekatherina. I've made my decision, and of everyone, you're the one I need in my corner."

Evangeline flushed. After these past years of tagging along, forcing herself into the mix of her brother's life, she'd never known how he felt about her, or any of it. "Then I'm in your corner."

"Good." Augustus returned his full focus to his work. The conversation was over.

And that was that.

Now, days later, she'd seen him even less than usual. The holidays were slower at the office, because their holiday edition had been off to press for weeks already. This was his time to relax and come home, if not on time, at least not past midnight.

Evangeline had noted, in the scientific journal of her mind, that her brother's hours worked per week climbed in direct correlation with his anxiety. But it didn't take a scientific journal, or mind, to see that the cause of his anxiety was self-imposed and therefore entirely baffling.

If he was so stressed at the idea of marrying the girl, then why was he? Because he didn't think he could do better? Because her expectations weren't so high of him as other women's might be? Because he thought he must?

Evangeline toyed with the idea that he'd accidentally gotten her pregnant, but she summarily dismissed it as quickly as it appeared. The girl was sleeping in the guest room. They'd never even sealed the deal, she'd bet her trust fund.

And now it was Christmas Eve, and she had no helpful answers on the subject of her brother's impending marriage, nor did she have any idea if she'd even see him on Christmas.

The family had been unraveling since the death of Madeline.

No, this started earlier. Way earlier.

Nothing had been right since their father died.

There was someone she could talk to about this. Not Colleen, because she could see now that to help her big sister she needed to shoulder some of the burden for a spell. When Colleen was better, she'd come and take over, but for now, Evangeline had to tend to the health and well-being of her family, though she was already off to a piss-poor start.

Amnesty. Her heart sank into the oak floorboards. Everything had been going so well, the two of them wrapped in the magic of late nights and no expectations. For months, and then... nothing. Two weeks ago, Amnesty hadn't showed up. Evangeline was disappointed, but not yet worried. Perhaps she was sick, or she'd turned in early. Amnesty didn't owe her an explanation for a night off.

But one turned to two, and two to a week. By the start of the second week, Evangeline dismissed any reasonable explanations, and her thoughts turned to fear. Had something terrible happened? She felt she knew Amnesty in a way she'd never known another living soul, though she knew almost nothing about her. It was crazy, but true, and she spent the next two days working up the courage to knock on the door and ask after her.

The wrought iron gate had been locked, so she nimbly scaled the spikes, using a nearby tree branch to pull herself up and then over. The yard was a mess. The gardens and lawn hadn't been tended in many years. All this had been blocked by those passing by, because Amnesty's grandfather, or whoever managed the gardeners, had ensured the outward appearances were maintained. Now that Evangeline was in their world, she was overcome with a sharp fear, and a sense that she was an interloper. Her eyes darted around the overgrown property, and behind her, as if expecting an apex predator to overtake her at any moment.

The steps bowed inward at the center, and one was missing entirely. She stretched over and beyond it, to the porch, which creaked under her tender weight.

Cobwebs wrapped themselves around the knocker, which belied the breadth of years passed since a time where it was in use; where the house and the world around it pulsed with life.

Evangeline ignored the nest of old world madness and knocked against the peeling wood door. She leaned in to listen and heard nothing. None of the familiar steps or stomps of approaching hosts. She knocked again, and then again, and as she was giving up, the large door yawned open.

An old man, beset with heavy arthritis and age spots, appeared. He hunched over his cane with the shakes. "Get off my porch before I call the police!"

"I'm not an intruder!" Evangeline put her hands up. "I'm just looking for Amnesty. I haven't seen her in a week and—"

"No one here by that name!"

"Are you sure? Maybe you call her something else? I've seen her come home every night after our walks."

"No one lives here but me, and no one is allowed here but me, and if you don't leave right this minute, I'll—"

"Yeah, I got it, call the police," Evangeline replied, confused, deflated.

The old man watched her like a preying hawk, huffing and tapping his cane while she went back down the path. She was able to unlock the gate from the inside and went out the proper way. The sound of first the gate locking itself, and then the heavy door closing rang in near unison, and she continued to replay the sounds on the long walk home.

Tomorrow was Christmas, and she didn't know where she'd be. Where she'd be, or where she belonged, and now she wasn't at all sure if the two were even the same. She'd floated from Ophélie to Magnolia Grace, and now Augustus was marrying and she was still aimless and incomplete.

Evangeline sighed in the dark, quiet house. The soft, mechanical tick of the grandfather clock was the dominant sound in a mansion of creaks and cries. She didn't want to be alone, but she didn't have it in her to call Augustus and ask him to come home just to appease her childish emotions.

A series of creaks in close succession raised her to alert. The house was always yawning and settling. It never slept. But these were the sounds of something growing closer, and she turned toward the direction of it. The porch.

Someone was outside.

Evangeline stood completely still. She strained to listen. The footsteps continued and then stopped. The metallic squeak of the porch swing came next.

It wasn't Augustus. She couldn't even begin to imagine him doing something as whimsical and without purpose as *swinging*. He probably didn't even know the thing was there.

Evangeline glanced around for something she could wield. The fireplace was nearby, but had no poker—just one, of many, things her brother had never used—and all she could find was an umbrella. She almost laughed. Might as well be a spoon.

She considered calling the police, but the risk of looking like a fool exceeded her fears of personal safety. In all likelihood, it was a bum who'd wandered up from the wharves, or Central City. None of the homeless in New Orleans had ever caused her trouble, and more than once she'd taken them into a nearby restaurant for a hot meal. Augustus would ream her if she let one in his house, but she had twenty dollars in her pocket, and that would be enough to change someone's life, if only for a week.

Evangeline removed the fasteners on the locks and turned the handle. The swing stopped. She took a deep breath and popped out, umbrella brandished.

Amnesty was curled into a corner of the swing. The moonlight revealed enough of her face that Evangeline could see the bruising around her left eye and her swollen lip. Her arms wrapped around her legs, and she looked tiny, like a forgotten child.

Evangeline dropped the umbrella. She stepped closer and perched at the other end of the swing. "What—"

"Don't ask me what happened, Evangeline. I can't tell you."

"Okay." Evangeline exhaled. She wrapped her thick hair in her fist and released it. "Okay."

"You want to ask me so many things."

"I've always wanted to."

"You want to know me."

"I already do know you, and then also, I don't know you at all."

"No one does."

Evangeline bowed her head.

"Okay, one question, but not about this." Amnesty pointed at her face. "But anything else. Ask me, and I'll tell you the truth."

"You don't live in that house on St. Charles, do you?" Evangeline blurted, before she realized she had so many other questions whose answers she desired more.

"No, and I think you just wasted your question. I'm a fair person. I'll give you one more."

Evangeline leaned forward over her folded hands. Some questions weren't yet in a place to be asked... other questions needed to come first... and yet others, once asked, couldn't be unasked. "You came to me for a reason."

Amnesty smiled. She winced as her lips stretched the gaping cut. "That's not a question."

"I don't know how to ask it," Evangeline admitted.

Amnesty unfolded her gangly limbs from the cocoon of safety and crawled across the swaying swing until she was lying across Evangeline's lap.

"Then just hold me," she said as she drew her legs up to her chest, and Evangeline's hand rested against her flesh.

CHARLES PACED the long hallway at the base of the stairs at Ophélie. His bottle of Hennessy swung with careless sweeps, back and forth, the occasional spray staining the cypress.

He wasn't going to answer the door. He didn't have to. Was he not the master of this fucking house? The master of this whole fucking family? No one made him do a goddamn thing, not now, not ever.

"Charles, please. Let me in."

"Go home to your husband!" he slurred. He wasn't that drunk, but it made him feel better to sound as if he'd abandoned all his senses to the booze. It wasn't for lack of trying. He'd realized, too late, long after the liquor stores in driving distance were closed, that he was dry. This last holdout bottle of cognac he found buried in his duffle bag, but it was half-drunk and it wouldn't be enough.

"Please, Charles. It's Christmas."

"Christmas Eve."

"I came all this way."

"Bully for you!" Charles took a healthy swig of the amber liquid and enjoyed the burn as it traveled southward.

"Darling." Her voice dropped. He heard her lean into the door. "Please. Do this for me."

Charles didn't will his hand to release the lock, and later wondered what the hell his brain had been thinking, sending signals to limbs as if it, and not he, were in control here.

Catherine stood wrapped in her pink pea coat, looking far more a woman now than she ever had. She held her arms close to her body, and when she removed her gloves, a present appeared.

"This is for you."

"I don't want it," he barked.

"I know you don't, but I want you to have it." Catherine closed the door behind her. She tended to her jacket, gloves, and purse, slow, dainty, like a woman entering a tea party.

"I didn't let you in."

Catherine smiled. "Yes you did."

"Not intentionally."

"Still. I'm here." She wrung her hands over the torso of her dress that Charles could only describe as "Jackie O," a cross between a stewardess and old Jack's wife. Only thing missing was a pillbox hat.

"You sure the fuck are," Charles drawled. "You're here, and your husband is back home. Does he know where you've gone?"

"You know the answer to that."

Charles wagged his index finger. The others were wound through the small handle on the bottle. "And *that* is a good test. If you can't tell the old man where you've gone, you probably shouldn't go."

"You're not one to give advice on life choices," Catherine said.

"Being a hypocrite doesn't make me wrong."

She smiled. "You're right."

"Why are you here?" Why *was* she here? Why had she ever been here?

"I wanted to wish you a Merry Christmas."

Charles spat on the floor. "Bullshit."

"Why are you alone?"

"Preparing the family home for my future wife and whatever mutant children she manages to produce in her toxic womb. Why are you *here*, Cat?"

Cat dropped her eyes to her twiddling fingers. "I suppose I don't really know."

"That's not good enough."

"For who?"

For me. "For your husband at home who trusts you, and has no fucking clue that you keep playing with fire."

"I love Colin," she said, "but it's not... you know..."

"No, I don't know. I don't fucking know. I will *never* fucking know, because your speech about security and safety didn't make me feel better, it made me feel worse! Because all that sob story only for me to feel like I can't give you that. What kind of man do you think I am that you decided for me that *I couldn't give you that*?"

Cat's face was covered in sadness. "It wasn't that I didn't think you could. I just didn't think you would want to."

"That I wouldn't want to?" Charles chewed his knuckle, then ran the back of his hand up over his forehead before slapping his skull. "Why did you get to decide what I want and don't want?"

Her shoulders lifted in a weak shrug. "Can you blame me? I've known you long enough to know what puts a fire in your belly, Charles Deschanel. How many times did you brag to Colin and me about your dating rules? You're a proud man, and by listening to you, one would think you were most proud of the notches on your belt."

Charles scoffed. He swallowed another swig of Hennessy.

"I know you were with other girls, when you were with me," Catherine said.

"No, Catherine, I wasn't." He closed his eyes. "In the beginning I was, but not later."

"I wasn't mad... after all, I was the one who wanted to keep what we had between us. But when I knew I'd fallen for you, I was scared to death."

"Scared? Of me?"

"Of loving a man who wasn't capable of loving me back."

Charles tossed the empty bottle aside. He charged forward, and when she recoiled, he gasped and stopped in place. "*I have never loved anyone in my whole life but you, Catherine Connelly!*"

Silent tears cut a path down her cheeks. "I think Shakespeare wrote a story about this."

"Oh, not *that* fucking guy," Charles hissed. He covered his face with both hands. "Why are you here? Why are you torturing us both?"

Catherine's soft hands peeled his away. Her lips fell on his. "I try," she said. Her tongue ran across the spot where his lips had been. "I force myself not to think of you. Of how you touched me... the way you brought out the best in who I was, and who I wanted to be. With you, I was the Cat in Paris writing poetry. I was the free spirit, unafraid of the world. I told myself the cost of feeling this way was my heartbreak when you inevitably let me down. But it was me who let you down instead."

Charles ran his thumbs over the tops of her hands. Her skin felt like silk against his rough touch. "Not everything in life works out," he said. He brought both her hands to his lips and kissed them each, one by one. "But I know one thing for sure."

"What?"

Charles lowered her hands back to her sides. He took a step back. "I can't get over you if you keep showing up, with your heart in your damn hands."

"My heart is yours, though. I can't help it. God help me, I wish I could, but I can't."

"I'm giving it back." Charles dug his hands into his pockets before he could put them somewhere else, somewhere more dangerous for his head and heart. "It's not mine anymore."

"It will always be yours."

Charles' eyes burned, but he wouldn't fucking allow it. "I don't accept this gift anymore, Catherine. Go home. Go home to Colin."

Catherine bowed her head and sobbed.

Charles opened the door. He didn't look at her, he couldn't. But he had to say this, because if he didn't, he would risk now and always wanting to walk back through the door she held perpetually half-open for him.

"I love you, Catherine. I loved you from the first time you smiled at me, and I'll love you until the day God takes me away. And it's because of that love that we're done here. I love you too much to let you ruin your life, and Colin's, for something that will never, ever be. You're not mine, and next time you come knocking, I won't answer. I won't be here. Not ever again."

Charles gently nudged her out the door and closed it behind her. "Merry Christmas, Catherine. This is the most important gift you'll ever receive."

He climbed the stairs, dragging himself up by the bannister, one by one, and collapsed in a heap at the top.

EPILOGUE: IRISH COLLEEN AND THE SEVEN

Colleen Deschanel, known as Irish Colleen to her family and friends, walked past the faces of her seven children, as she did every night of her life.

It was Christmas, the most sacred day in their household, but after dinner they'd scattered back to their lives, such as they were. This new house, smaller, less welcoming and cozy than all they'd known before it, was *a* home, but it did not yet feel like *her* home. And it would never, ever be *their* home.

They were a house divided now. Hardly more than a year ago, they'd all been under the same roof, all except her sweet Madeline, who was with God now. Augustus had left first, then Evangeline. Colleen had announced her intentions to leave not only the family home, but the country, for a program that would keep her away for years. It had been Irish Colleen's decision to leave Ophélie with Maureen and Elizabeth, to allow Charles to begin his life as a new man, before marriage tied him down, but she was allowed to be sad about it.

All seven of her children lined the marble mantle of the townhouse that would be her home now, and possibly always.

Charles. Her heir. Her darling boy, and her reckless, impulsive failure. He was both, and he was neither, and she loved him so fiercely that his indiscretions carved large gashes in her heart, which now held scores of ticks and tacks. Of all her resentments toward her late husband, his terrible judgment the day Franz Hendrickson killed John Hannaford sat at the very top. Charles had wanted to know the story so badly, and Irish Colleen couldn't blame him, but there was no satisfying answer. Charles' father had made a bed that Charles now had to lie in, and his road ahead would be fraught with joyless struggle.

He blamed her, too. For going along with August's wishes, long after he'd died. For giving in to a blackmailer. But life had taught Irish Colleen a lesson Charles might never learn. The universe was not so evenly balanced between good and evil. God had given them so much evil to contend with as a test of faith and pulled back the goodness so they might prove their faith under duress. But Charles had no faith, and so he would have none of the comfort faith provided in the days ahead.

Augustus had just that evening shared his blessed news. Irish Colleen had always feared the most for the happiness of her second son. He'd never been as impassioned as the others. Even Colleen had her desires. Augustus went through life with all the outward signs of a man with a passion, but Irish Colleen, as disconnected as she might be with the finer edges of emotion, understood he was going through the motions, as if one day he might wake up and find himself happy quite by accident.

Ekatherina had been there, at his side. She was a slight, nervous thing who said five words the entire evening. Her eyes lit up as she watched the others open their gifts and gather around the tree and hearth, and Irish Colleen thought she understood the girl for a moment. Family was her spark, and Augustus could give her that, even if he himself had never been sparked by anything real. He mentioned to her in passing that he was determined to bring Ekatherina's family here from Russia, but she suspected the path to do so would be harder than he was expecting.

Colleen floated from house to house. She would stay at one until she grew restless, no more than a few nights, and rotate to another. She'd had news of her own on Christmas. Her dates for Scotland had moved up. There was no explanation given for why the change, and Irish Colleen didn't ask. This was what her daughter needed. She'd do nothing, say nothing, to jeopardize that.

Colleen would be leaving her, soon. Very soon. And if she was smart, she would never, ever come back.

Irish Colleen turned around and looked at her middle daughter. Evangeline had fallen asleep on the couch before Augustus left with his fiancée. She didn't want to go home with them, not that she'd said anything of the sort. Irish Colleen sensed the turmoil in Evangeline; had always sensed it, but lacked the skills to address or soothe her pain. She'd wake soon and say, groggy, "I didn't mean to fall asleep," but they'd both know this wasn't true. Irish Colleen would kiss her on the forehead and assure her this was her home, too. This townhouse wasn't much, but her children were welcome without question, now as always.

Irish Colleen gave one last longing glance to the mantle. Madeline's troubled face, framed by her beautiful mahogany hair, smiled back at her, and she closed her eyes. Her prayer for her daughter was between her and God.

She started up the stairs, to where the bedrooms lined the hall in a neat row.

Maureen snored softly from her daybed. Had she done the right thing, bringing her troubled child back to New Orleans? Maureen had been doing so well at Ophélie, minus a few bumps in the road. She'd even become something of a student. And now, she'd pulled her back into the lion's den. Maureen didn't know her mother was aware of the Virgins Only Club, just as the other children assumed Irish Colleen was an old, blind fool. But she didn't miss much. She wasn't so very different from Ophelia in that way.

Irish Colleen blew Maureen a kiss and closed the door with a gentle click.

She hadn't told Elizabeth to pick the room at the end of the hall. Lizzy had chosen it herself, as she had in their old New Orleans mansion, and later at Ophélie. She gravitated toward the farthest space from the rest of the living, as though there was protection in being alone.

Elizabeth was awake and crying. She was no longer the waif drowning in her soaked nightgown, but a young woman now, with breasts and curves, and soft lines around her smiles. She was nearing an age where Irish Colleen might have to stop her daughter and Connor from being alone together in the bedroom, but she hadn't the heart to take Elizabeth's single joy in life and taint it with the stench of insinuation.

Irish Colleen didn't ask her daughter what was wrong. This day would forever and always be the bridge between what was and whatever lay against the horizon, waiting.

"You can talk to me, Lizzy."

"I know, Mama." Elizabeth crossed her arms over her chest. She was at the age where she'd become self-conscious of all the tell-tale signs of her passing over to womanhood.

"This was a strange Christmas. But God has deemed it time for some of our family to begin new lives, and He will provide."

Elizabeth curled her mouth in a sardonic smile. "God had nothing to do with Franz Hendrickson killing John Hannaford and sealing Charles' fate with that wretched hag."

"You know about that?"

Elizabeth laughed. "We're not blind to your secrets, Mama, any more than you're blind to ours."

Irish Colleen pulled her shoulders back with a small *hmph*. "Charles will find his way."

"If you say so."

"If there's something you want to say, be direct, Lizzy."

"What can I say, Mama? You don't need my visions to tell you Charles will be miserable. Cordelia is only the beginning."

"That's all you'll tell me?"

"You don't want to know more." Elizabeth pulled her long blond hair over one shoulder. "You always ask, but I know your limits."

"Elizabeth, who is the mother here, pray?"

Elizabeth laughed. Irish Colleen joined in after a too-serious pause.

"The truth is, I never see anything but pain," Elizabeth said when the brief joy died away into the night. "I asked *Tante* Ophelia if this is what she saw, too, and her visions are more balanced than mine. She thinks mine will become that way, but what if they never do? Every Christmas, Mama, you ask me what the next year will bring, and every year I tell you that the sadness ahead is more than we've ever known. And every year this is true. Next year will be our worst year yet."

"Why, Elizabeth?"

"Charles and Augustus..." Elizabeth shook her head. "No, not this time, Mama. I can't give this to others anymore."

"Doesn't it help to relieve the burden?"

Elizabeth shook her head. Her hair slipped back down her back. "Not anymore."

Irish Colleen closed her eyes and said a silent prayer for her baby.

"Not with what's coming for us," Elizabeth finished.

The End
Forest Grove, OR
August 11, 2018 11:45 a.m.

ALSO BY SARAH M. CRADIT

THE SAGA OF CRIMSON & CLOVER

The Seven Series:

1970

1972

1973

1974

1975

1976

1980

Midnight Dynasty Series:

A Tempest of Discovery

The House of Crimson and Clover Series:

This is the recommended reading order of the series.

The Storm and the Darkness

Shattered

The Illusions of Eventide

Bound

Midnight Dynasty

Asunder

Empire of Shadows

Myths of Midwinter

The Hinterland Veil

The Secrets Amongst the Cypress

Within the Garden of Twilight

House of Dusk, House of Dawn

Vampires of the Merovingi Series

The Island

Crimson & Clover Lagniappes (Bonus Stories):

Lagniappes are standalone stories that can be read in any order.

St. Charles at Dusk: The Story of Oz and Adrienne

Flourish: The Story of Anne Fontaine

Surrender: The Story of Oz and Anasofiya

Shame: The Story of Jonathan St. Andrews

Fire & Ice: Remy & Fleur Fontenot

Dark Blessing: The Landry Triplets

Pandora's Box: Jasper and Pandora Broussard

The Menagerie: Cyler

A Band of Heather: Colleen and Noah

The Ephemeral: Autumn Sullivan

Banshee: The Story of Giselle Deschanel

For more information, and exciting bonus material, visit www.sarahmcradit.com

THE FAMILY

Deschanel Family (Line of August)

The Deschanel (*pronounced Day-shah-nell*) family are the line of heirs of the great Charles Deschanel of France, who settled the Deschanel dynasty in Louisiana in 1844. All current day descendants of this original Charles are either of the line of August or Blanche. Deschanels are of the line of August, and all others (Fontenots, Broussards, Guidrys, etc.) come from Blanche. August, with his wife "Irish" Colleen Brady, had seven children: Charles, Augustus, Colleen, Madeline, Evangeline, Maureen, and Elizabeth. Madeline, their fourth child, tragically passed in an automobile accident on Christmas morning, 1970.

Irish Colleen was August's second wife. His first, Eliza, he married for love, but she was unable to bear children and eventually passed away from cancer.

The rights of inheritance of the Deschanels follow the tradition of the eldest son, so Charles, son of August, is the current heir.

August (1905-1961) & "Irish" Colleen Brady (1932-)

Charles b. 1950
Augustus b. 1951
Colleen b. 1952
Madeline b. 1953
Evangeline b. 1954
Maureen b. 1956
Elizabeth b. 1959

Deschanel-Broussard Family (Line of Blanche)

The Deschanel-Broussard family (*pronounced Brew-sard*), are cousins of the Deschanel family, equal in wealth and prestige. Where the Deschanels are descendants of the line of August, the Broussards are descendants of the line of Blanche. Claudius Broussard is Blanche's third husband, and the children from this union are considered her most favored. She also has a son by her second husband, Johnson Guidry, but her relationship with Pierce is fractured.

Blanche did not have children by her first husband, Ellis Kenner. Both Ellis Kenner and Johnson Guidry died of "mysterious circumstances."

Blanche Deschanel (b. 1906) & Johnson Guidry (1890-1930)

Pierce b. 1926

& Claudius Broussard (b. 1900)

Eugenia b. 1940
Pierce b. 1926
Cassius b. 1942
Wyatt (1943-1955)
Noble (1944-1955)

Guidry Family (Line of Blanche)

The Guidry family are those descended from Pierce Guidry, first son of Blanche Deschanel-Broussard. Although the first son is the heir on the Deschanel side, Blanche does not recognize Pierce as her heir. Instead, she sees her second child and eldest daughter, Eugenia Fontenot, as her heir. Pierce represents his line of the family as one of the seven Deschanel Magi Collective Council. His two daughters, Pansy and Kitty, are also on the Council.

Of Pierce's children, only Pansy, so far, is married.

The Guidrys, for no reason other than Blanche's disdain for her second husband, Johnson, are considered the black sheep of the clan.

Pierce Guidry (b. 1926) & Winnifred Babin (b. 1926)

Pansy b. 1949 (m. Placide Lafont b. 1945)
Alton b. 1950
Kitty b. 1954

Fontenot Family (Line of Blanche)

The Fontenot family are those descended from Eugenia Broussard-Fontenot, second daughter of Blanche Deschanel-Broussard. Although Eugenia is a second child, and a daughter to boot, Blanche recognizes Eugenia as her heir. Eugenia is married to Wallace Fontenot, and they have three sons. Eugenia represents her line of the family as one of the seven Deschanel Magi Collective Council.

The Fontenots are well-respected in the community, with a similar prestige as their Deschanel cousins.

Eugenia Broussard (b. 1940) & Wallace Fontenot (b. 1939)

Luther b. 1962
Llewellyn b. 1963
Lowell b. 1964

Broussard Family (Line of Blanche)

The Broussard family are those descended from Cassius, third child and second son of Blanche Deschanel-Broussard. Cassius is married to Helene Barrow, and they have two children, a son and a daughter. Cassius represents his line of the family as one of the seven Deschanel Magi Collective Council.

The Broussards, like the Fontenots, are well-respected in the community, with a similar prestige as their Deschanel cousins.

Cassius Broussard (b. 1942) & Helene Barrow (b. 1944)

Jasper b. 1963

Imogen b. 1965

Sullivan Family

The Sullivans are one of the oldest and most trusted families in New Orleans. A family of attorneys, a majority of Sullivans, most notably males until recently, join the family law firm, Sullivan & Associates, which has been a New Orleans staple since 1839. The family came up through the ranks, by their bootstraps, with humble beginnings as Irish immigrant laborers. The Sullivans are both the attorneys and friends of the Deschanel Family. Like the Deschanels, the designation of heir follows the eldest son, and so Colin Sullivan Sr. is considered the head of the family. His father, Patrick, still lives, but in quiet retirement.

Colin Sullivan Sr. (b. 1932) & Josephine Bartleby (b. 1931)

Colin Sullivan Jr. b. 1950

Rory Sullivan b. 1952

Patrick Sullivan b. 1953

Chelsea Sullivan b. 1956

Sullivan & Associates

Sullivan & Associates is a family-owned law firm, and one of the oldest and most trusted in New Orleans, founded in 1839 by Aidan Sullivan. Comprised mostly of Sullivans, the firm is considered something of a birthright for any Sullivans looking to go into law. They have represented the Deschanel interests for over a century. Charles Deschanel's best friend, Colin Sullivan Jr., as well as Colin's two brothers, Rory and Patrick, all plan to join the family firm one day. Colin Sullivan Sr. is the current Senior Partner, following the retirement of his father, Patrick. Colin Sr. and his brothers, Jerome and Jamie, are the figureheads of the firm.

HOMES & PROPERTIES

Oak Haven

The old Victorian mansion Irish Colleen and seven used to live in, on Chestnut and Sixth in the Garden District, just beyond Lafayette Cemetery No. 1. Although there are larger (Magnolia Grace) and more storied (Ophélie) homes in the family possession, August Deschanel chose this particular property to raise his family in with the thought of giving them a more "normal" upbringing than he had.

The Gardens

The colossal mansion of Ophelia Deschanel at Jackson Ave., taking up an entire square block between Coliseum and Prytania in the Garden District. The Gardens also houses the cavernous chambers where the Deschanel Magi Collective and the Collective Council meet to discuss family business. The architectural style of the estate is Italianate, and the most notable feature is the extensive, exotic garden wrapping around the property, shielding the home from outside view. This house will be inherited by the future Deschanel Magi Collective Magistrate.

Ophélie

A large plantation and surrounding lands purchased by Charles Deschanel I, built in 1844, and currently occupied intermittently by the Deschanel family. Charles will inherit the property as the heir to the estate. Located near Vacherie, an hour west of New Orleans, the Greek Revival ivory mansion on the Mississippi River is secluded from the road by gates and foliage. The estate has forty-five rooms and large ornate gardens, as well as two hundred outbuildings from when the property was a working plantation.

Magnolia Grace

A beautiful, traditional Greek Revival mansion in the Garden District that once belonged to Fitz Deschanel (the second son of Charles I), and has ever since been passed down through the second sons. Augustus Deschanel inherited this property, which is located on Prytania, near Eighth.

Deschanel Media Group

The brainchild of Augustus Deschanel, who had dreamed of starting his own company since he was a young boy. The company's vision is a magazine for locals, which both catered to the elites but also offered an opportunity for aspiring writers to get their short stories published and in front of potential patrons.

Femme Forte

A sprawling Northshore mansion along Lake Pontchartrain, considered the birthright of Blanche and her descendants. The property will be inherited by Eugenia Fontenot, her favorite child.

Weatherly Estate

The vast, columned Uptown home of Daniel Weatherly Sr., gifted for his patronage of Tulane. His son, Dan Jr., is a good friend of Charles Deschanel. The estate is located near the sister universities of Tulane and Loyola, by the Ursuline's Academy.

ABOUT THE AUTHOR

Sarah is the *USA Today* Bestselling Author of the Paranormal Southern Gothic world, The Saga of Crimson & Clover, born of her combined passion for New Orleans, and the mysterious complexity of human nature. Her work has been described as rich, emotive, and highly dimensional.

An unabashed geek, Sarah enjoys studying obscure subjects like the Plantagenet and Ptolemaic dynasties, and settling debates on provocative Tolkien topics such as why the Great Eagles are not Gandalf's personal taxi service. Passionate about travel, Sarah has visited over twenty countries collecting sparks of inspiration (though New Orleans is where her heart rests). She's a self-professed expert at crafting original songs to sing to her very patient pets, and a seasoned professional at finding ways to humiliate herself (bonus points if it happens in public). When at home in Oregon, her husband and best friend, James, is very kind about indulging her love of fast German cars and expensive lattes.

www.sarahmcradit.com

Made in the USA
Lexington, KY
07 April 2019